JEREMIAH'S DAUGHTER (AMISH ROMANCE)

BOOK 6 AMISH MISFITS

SAMANTHA PRICE

Purple Palm Press

CHAPTER 1

Beverly Beiler had vowed she'd never go back to her childhood Amish community in New York's Conewango Valley. She had meant every word. Returning for her father's funeral might have been the only conceivable reason, but *Dat* was very much alive. Incapacitated with a broken leg, but still alive. It was the shock of her father calling after no word in ten years that prompted her to come home. He'd asked if she'd come and help with the bed-and-breakfast.

Beverly wasted no time in asking for

leave from her job at the bank and booking a ticket on the bus. The major drawback about her hasty decision to help was having to see Janet again.

Beverly's parents were old when she was born. They were so old to be having their first child that folks in the community used to joke about them being like Sarah and Abraham from the Bible. Her mother had been in her late forties then, and she'd died when Beverly was just eleven. Her father had been even older, in his fifties when she was born. Now her father was eighty and had been married to Janet, his second wife, for many years. She was a most objectionable woman, the cause of Beverly fleeing the community at eighteen.

What would her mother have thought about Janet? That was something Beverly had often wondered.

Beverly was relieved to be off the bus and in a taxi. It was six hours from New York

City and going by bus always made things seem that much longer. It was times like these she wished she owned a car, but parking was too limited in the city and her apartment didn't come with a car space. Only the highly priced apartments came with those.

Soon she'd be at the restored and extended farmhouse, which Janet had encouraged Jeremiah to convert to a bed-and-breakfast not long after they married. As she passed by the Amish farmlands, Beverly's stomach churned. From the back seat, she leaned over toward the driver. "Can we stop a moment?"

The driver grumbled something she couldn't understand, and then pulled off the road.

"Thanks. I just need to walk up and down for a moment." He didn't answer. Either that or she'd been too quick to jump out to hear his response. She held onto her tummy as she walked, wondering if it had been a bad idea to come back.

The phone call from her father replayed in her mind. He explained he'd been fixing the roof when he'd fallen off and broken his leg. Well aware he could've died, she probed further and then found out the real reason behind his call. It was the financial problems they were having. He went on to ask if she would help Janet out while he was bed-bound.

Naturally, her first response was to ask if Janet was in agreement. He assured her she was. For some reason, her father had confidence Beverly could pull them out of their debt. Was it just an excuse to see her again? It could've been. It pleased her that he'd called when he found himself in trouble, but at the same time, what if she'd needed him? She'd written to him over the years telling him of her success in the banking arena, but he'd never replied to any of her letters.

In their brief conversation, he said he was confident she'd be able to figure out why the number of visitors had dwindled away. It seemed odd that Janet would be in agreement with her coming back to help—a further sign of how bad things were.

Now glancing back at the taxi, she was aware that the meter was tick-tick-ticking away. Then the thought occurred to her that the driver could simply drive off with her suitcase in the trunk and the handbag she'd left in the back seat. All her valuables were in that handbag—her cell phone and driver's license, and her diamond engagement ring. Squinting hard at the driver, she saw him holding a phone up to his ear; he didn't look as though he was going anywhere. With one reluctant step after the other, she made her way back to the car.

The driver promptly ended his call just as she opened the door. "Good to go?" he asked.

Obviously, he was a man of few words,

but at least he wasn't mumbling this time. "Yes, thanks." She pushed her long strawberry blonde hair back, tucking it behind her ears. It had fallen over her face from the breeze, as usual. She held her stomach tightly as the car drove on. And then a calm sensation washed over her and all tension melted away. She felt her mother's comforting presence right beside her in the backseat of the taxi. It was a strange sensation, one she'd never had before, and she savored it.

Then the taxi rounded the corner, and there it was. The large white two-level house still had the familiar red roof and the large red barn close by. It was the house where she'd been born. Memories of her mother singing hymns while she breezed through the daily chores hummed through her mind, as did visions of her father telling her bible stories at night. Her favorite had been about Daniel in the lion's den. With having to face

Janet, she was about to enter the lions' den for real.

BEVERLY'S MIND drifted to days gone by, growing up in this house and smelling the delicious food her mother always made. Four days a week there was the aroma of her warm fresh bread, and back then that was Beverly's favorite food and she'd preferred to eat it just as it came out of the oven.

Her mother always made things fun. On Saturdays, her closest friends, Betsy and Leah, would come to the house and they'd all help her mother make popcorn balls and taffy apples. Then while they played, her mother would make them sandwiches and they'd take them to the field and there they'd have a picnic. Those were Beverly's fondest memories.

When Beverly remained in the taxi after

it stopped, the driver turned around. "This is the address you gave me."

"Yes. Thank you."

She failed to move, and he added, "Is it the right place?"

"Yes. I need a moment." She wanted to look her best so she took out the lip balm from her handbag and, with the tip of a fingernail, carefully dotted it over her dry lips. Janet would faint if she saw painted lips and probably wouldn't let her in the house. That's why she'd worn no makeup at all and, with her fair skin and light-colored lashes, she knew she looked as pale as a ghost. But still, there'd be no one to see her, only Janet and her father and they were used to seeing her unmade-up natural face.

The driver jumped out of the car to get her suitcase out of the truck.

When she finally got out, the driver stood there with her suitcase on the ground, waiting to be paid.

"Thank you." Beverly gave him the amount she'd seen on the meter and then some. That made him smile.

"Do you want me to carry your bag in for you?"

"No, it's fine there, thanks."

He wasted no time getting in the car and zooming away. Beverly made herself pick up her bag and move forward. When she got closer to the house, she saw it looked a little rundown and, sadly, her mother's much-loved garden was now overgrown.

When her foot landed on the first step of the porch, the front door swung open and out stepped Janet. Beverly froze to the spot and their eyes locked.

Janet still wore the same dissatisfied expression as she had the day Beverly left all those years ago—it seemed like a lifetime ago. In many ways it was. Janet's dark piercing eyes were just as beady and wisps of white hair like spirals of smoke from a chimney framed her gaunt face. She reminded Beverly of a storybook witch, or the wicked step-mother in a story, but this was no fairy-tale. There were no wicked stepsisters, and alas, no handsome prince was waiting to whisk her away to his palace high on a mountaintop.

Right this moment, Beverly was painfully aware of one thing—her long hot-pink acrylic fingernails. She'd not worn makeup, but had overlooked her nails. Trying to hide them, she put one hand behind her back and the other she tucked further around the handle of her suitcase.

"You came after all." Janet said, her expression unchanged. She still wore that permanent pout of disapproval.

It was going to be a long four weeks. "I told *Dat* I was coming."

Janet made a sound, much like a scoff.

"How is he?" Beverly wondered if she should turn around and head back home.

With Janet there, she'd always feel like an outsider. With a quick glance over her shoulder, she saw the taxi was nowhere in sight. She looked back at Janet.

"He's not well. That's why he called you. Come in. You're not going to be any good to him if you don't come inside."

Beverly swallowed hard and walked up the rest of the steps. "Where should I put my bag?" she asked once she was inside, deliberately ignoring the musty smell that permeated the home.

"You can stay in your old room, or wherever you want. It makes no difference since we have no bookings this week."

"I hope I can help with that. Where's *Dat*?"

"In his room."

That was probably the most she'd ever spoken to Janet in a whole day. Janet hurried off in the direction of the kitchen. The first

11

thing Beverly wanted to do was see her father.

Without wasting time, she hurried up the stairs to her old bedroom, opened the door and pushed her suitcase and handbag inside across the floor and pulled the door shut. The room held a lot of memories of her mother, and she decided she'd save her private memories for later.

Even though she hadn't seen her father in ten years, a sense of urgency took hold. As she made her way down the corridor, she recalled the last time she'd seen him. It was on the side of the road on the day she left, right after that huge argument with Janet.

Janet had told her to leave if she couldn't abide by her rules, and she couldn't abide by them. She'd packed her bag and, after a mouthful of newly-learned curse words, thanks to some newly-found questionable friends, she stomped away from the house. The only clothes she'd taken were a pair of jeans and a T-shirt that she'd bought in secret. Fortunately, she had money—five hundred and fifty dollars, her life savings from selling jams at roadside stalls with two of her friends over the previous two years.

Her father caught up with her when she was nearly at the bus stop. When she saw Jeremiah's buggy approaching, she was relieved and certain he was there to beg her to stay. A part of her hoped he would even say he was sending Janet away instead, but that wasn't to be. Instead, he handed her a small bag without speaking a word. She looked in the bag and saw lots of money. It confirmed to Beverly that they both knew she was never coming back. Beverly kept refusing to take it until her father told her that her mother would've wanted her to have it. She remembered his last and final words. *That money will be enough to take you somewhere nice and help you make a life for yourself.* She appreciated the gesture, but why couldn't he have chosen her over Janet?

She shrugged off the sadness of days gone by as she stood in front of Jeremiah's closed door. Gently, she knocked.

"Come in," came the quiet, almost-frail voice of her father.

She opened the door and saw him in bed, and then her eyes were drawn to the cast on his leg sitting atop the stack of folded blankets. Immediately her nostrils were assaulted by an unpleasant odor in the room, and going by the discoloration of the sheets she guessed they hadn't been changed in some time. Looking back at her father's smiling face, she couldn't' help being concerned about how aged and undernourished he appeared. The circles under his eyes were so dark they took on a magenta hue and his skin seemed thin and almost transparent.

Before she could speak or even take a second step into the room, Janet bustled past her. It was annoying. All Beverly wanted was a moment alone with her father. Doing her best to ignore her stepmother, she smiled back at her father. "Hello, *Dat.*"

Her father's face lit up even further. "Come closer. Is it really you?"

"Of course, it is. Who else would it be? I don't have a twin unless there's something you haven't told me."

Janet gasped as she stood at the foot of the bed. "What a dreadful thing to say."

"It was just a joke, Janet."

Her father agreed. "That's just Beverly's sense of humor."

"She's the only one to find it funny. So why is it funny anyway? I don't see that it is."

Her father ignored Janet's question. "Come closer," he repeated to Beverly. "It's been too long."

There was a lot Beverly wanted to say to him, but she wasn't comfortable with Janet standing there judging her every word. She glanced over at Janet. This was a perfect time to turn the tables. "When were these sheets last washed, Janet?"

"We must save on water. We have to save money wherever we can."

"Rubbish. This is a bed-and-breakfast. You must expect to spend a certain amount on water and other utilities. And why is this room so dark?"

"It's late in the afternoon. That's the way Jeremiah likes it. It keeps out the heat. It'll only get worse when we hit the middle of the summer."

Beverly walked three paces to the window and flung the curtains aside, and then opened the window.

"Fresh air is not good for someone when they're sick," Janet said.

"Are musty air and filthy dirty sheets good for the sick?"

"I'm not sick. I only have a broken leg. The sheets are—"

"And how long have you been wearing those pajamas?"

"Beverly, stop it! I can't listen to bickering. I didn't ask you here to cause trouble and fight with Janet. The two of you need to somehow get along because we're not going to survive if you don't."

Beverly looked at her father's distraught face and was ashamed of herself for upsetting him. She hadn't been there five minutes and she'd already had a row with Janet. While she was staying there, she had to put annoyance with Janet aside for the sake of her father. It wouldn't be easy, but she had to do it.

"If you'll stop talking and listen to me I'll tell you about the sheets."

"Go on."

"The sheets are yellowed because they're old. We use the old ones for ourselves and the better ones for the guests."

"Are things that bad?"

"Worse," Jeremiah said. "I was doing my own repairs around the place to save money and that's how I fell off the roof. I'm not as young as I used to be. I missed my footing. And then I came down."

"What can I do?" Beverly asked.

"Janet will show you the books. We can't understand why we're doing so poorly when others are thriving. I got your letters. I know you work in a bank."

"Why didn't you write back?"

He pushed his tongue into his cheek. After a pause, he said, "I don't know."

"I guess it doesn't matter now. Anyway, I've had a look on the Internet and you aren't listed with the major booking websites. That's a must."

"It can't be just that," he said.

"I'd say that's got a lot to do with it. I don't go on many vacations myself, but I know how my friends book all of their vacations. Can you show me the rooms, Janet?"

"Do you think it has something to do with the rooms?" Janet asked.

"It might. They might need an upgrade."

"And who's gonna pay for that?" Janet snapped.

"Stop it!" Jeremiah said. "Stop it the both of you. This bickering has to end now."

Beverly stopped herself from pointing out that she wasn't bickering at all. She was merely trying to find a way to help boost the numbers. "Sorry, *Dat.*" She didn't want to upset her father when he was helplessly lying in bed in between two women who loved him but couldn't stand each other. If Janet and Jeremiah had anyone else to turn to, they would've. She was a last resort and she knew it.

"Janet can show you the rooms and show you the figures after you settle in. How does that sound? You must be tired from your long trip."

"I am. Okay. That sounds good."

"Janet, why don't you make Beverly a nice cool glass of meadow tea?"

"It's too close to dinner."

"I'd love one thanks, Janet. I'm really not very hungry." Beverly smiled at Janet.

"I guess it wouldn't hurt," she said to Jeremiah, "Would you like one too?"

"*Jah.*"

When Janet left the room, her father held out his hand to Beverly. She clasped both of her hands around his. She wanted to apologise to him for being gone so long. Standing before him, she felt nothing but guilt. "What does the doctor say about your leg?"

"He says I'll live, at least a bit longer." His pale blue eyes twinkled. They were the same shade of blue as her own.

"I'm serious, *Dat*. Was it a bad break? You didn't tell me how bad it was on the phone."

"It wasn't a bad break. It didn't need to be pinned or anything. It'll mend in time."

"Can you get around on crutches?"

"*Jah,* I got some of those." He pointed to the other side of the room where they were propped up in the corner. "Janet doesn't like me getting around on them in case I fall."

"I'm sure you should try at least. And why aren't you in one of the downstairs bedrooms? Are you having physical therapy? You look a bit thin. Are you eating enough?"

"A lady stops by to do the therapy with me. She's stopping by soon, today. And, I'm eating plenty. And I'm more comfortable in this bed than downstairs."

"Are you doing everything the therapist says?"

"I can't do all she says. I do a little bit every day and that's all."

"*Dat,* that's very bad. You should do everything she says. That's the only way you'll recover speedily."

"If I fall, Janet won't be able to pull me off the floor."

Janet was a small, thin woman and her

father was nearly six feet tall. "That doesn't matter now that I'm here. When do you go back to the doctor's next?"

"Next week. I don't like doctors."

"I know you don't, but they do come in handy for things like broken legs," she said with a cheeky little grin.

He smiled up at her. *"Denke* for coming back, Beverly. I know it wasn't an easy thing to do."

"It wasn't. I took an extended vacation from work, and hopefully we'll be able to get the business on the way back to where it used to be before my leave is up."

He nodded, and then said, "Be careful what you say 'round Janet. She's sensitive."

"I'll do my best." She smiled at her father. What he'd said was comical. Janet was anything but sensitive.

"Good. I'd appreciate it."

Janet bustled back into the room with two tall glasses of meadow tea. It'd been a long time since Beverly had enjoyed the sweet minty taste of home-made Amish meadow tea.

When Janet saw their hands clasped together, she turned aside and placed the two glasses on the dresser on the other side of the room. Without saying anything, she stomped out of the room and closed the door behind her. It clearly upset Janet that Jeremiah had accepted her back so easily. Could Janet be jealous? Was that the reason why the woman was so sour?

"Maybe I shouldn't have come back," Beverly muttered as she walked across the room to retrieve the two glasses.

"Don't mind her. She has her moods. Every woman does."

"I don't know about that."

"Don't you?" He looked up at her with that same amused twinkle in his eyes. She was tempted to point out that what he'd said was sexist, but then she'd have to explain what that meant; she was far too tired for that.

"An extended vacation is four weeks long?" he asked.

"It's really six, but I took two weeks earlier in the year." She hoped he wouldn't ask what she'd done during those two weeks. She'd spent them with Kevin, and she no longer wanted to think about him.

Jeremiah pushed himself further up in the bed.

"Are you okay?" When he nodded, she handed him the glass.

Then she took a sip of her tea, and hoped she hadn't bitten off more than she could chew. She didn't know much about the day-to-day running of businesses. She knew about profit and loss statements and balance sheets and that was all.

After her father took a sip of tea, he sighed. "It's not as good as your *mudder* used to make it."

"*Dat,* you don't say things like that in front of Janet, do you?"

He opened his eyes wide. "It's not a lie."

"I'm not saying it is, but maybe, just maybe, a second wife doesn't want to be compared to the first one."

Her father looked away from her. "I see what you mean."

It sounded to Beverly like he might do that a bit. If Janet was constantly compared to her mother, it was no wonder the woman was so grim. "Have you finished with your drink?"

"I have for the moment."

Beverly took it from him and placed it on his nightstand. "It'll be here for you when you're ready." Then she noticed a bell. "What a cute little bell."

"*Jah,* I call Janet with that when I need her."

She picked up the bell and tinkled it. "Whoops, I shouldn't have done that. That'll bring Janet." Carefully, she replaced the bell where she'd found it.

When she looked back at her father, she saw his eyes close and his head drop to one side. Her heart jolted, nearly stopped, and she froze. Was he dead? Had she come all this way to see him take his last breath?

CHAPTER 2

SHE LOOKED CLOSER at his body for movement, and then heaved a sigh of relief when she saw the slight rise and fall of his chest.

Then he opened his eyes and looked at her. "We're in trouble, Petal."

She smiled at her father's pet name for her. No one had called her that since she had left. "That's why I'm here."

"Have you seen our books?"

Now she knew that there was more wrong with her father than just his leg. "Not yet. Janet is going to show me them soon." She regretted the time lost between them. It'd been wrong to let that woman stand in their way. At the time, living there had seemed impossible. Leaving had been her only reasonable choice. "Why don't you have a rest now, *Dat?* I'll find Janet and have a talk."

"Do your best to get along."

"I will. I'm older now and hopefully we're both more tolerant." She now wondered if Janet ever found out about that money father had given her. After six months of working at the bank, she'd been able to pay it back. It was a long time after he'd given it to her, but at least she paid it back, not that he'd asked her to do that. She felt it was the right thing to do. The sides of his mouth turned upward in a slight smile and she leaned over and kissed him on the forehead.

"It's good to see you again. I'm happy you're here."

"It's nice to see you again too." Neither of them had discussed the big issue of why she'd left. It was like that in her family. Things were always swept under the rug. Maybe it was best not to talk about things past and open old wounds. After another look back at her father, she walked away and left him alone. Downstairs, she found Janet in the kitchen. "I'm sorry, I've left my glass of tea up in the room."

"You always were forgetful."

"I'm still the same, I guess. I'll go fetch it." She turned to go back upstairs and then Janet said, "Forget it. I'll have to get Jeremiah's glass soon anyway. I can bring them all back on his dinner tray."

"Okay." As much as she didn't want to, she knew she'd have to find out from Janet what she was dealing with.

"Do you have time right now for us to talk?"

When Janet nodded, they both sat down at the kitchen table.

"Is *Dat* alright?"

"Did he belch badly again? It's just indigestion."

"No, it's not that. He seems a little vague."

Janet looked away from her. "He's been like that the last few months. I fear it's the first signs of dementia."

"Oh, that's not good."

Now Janet was looking back at her with those piercing eyes. *"Nee,* but it's *Gott's* will."

If there was one thing that annoyed Beverly it was saying that something was God's will. People had told her it was God's will when *Mamm* died. To this day, she still didn't understand how it was His will for her mother to leave her when she was so young. Beverly had been out of the community so long she'd forgotten how everything was considered God's will, good or bad. She didn't comment on the annoyance of it all and buried it deep inside along with all the other ideas that upset her. "How bad are things?"

"With the business?"

"Yes."

Janet sighed, and Beverly didn't know whether she was sighing because things were bad, or sighing because she'd just glanced at her stepdaughter's bright pink nails. "We're barely making enough to feed ourselves. And now we owe money we can't pay."

"When did things get so bad?"

Janet pushed a spiral of white hair back under her white *kapp.* "I'll tell you when. When two more places like this opened up not far from here. That's when the downturn began."

"Two more?"

Janet's dark eyes glistened with tears. *"Jah.* Two—one more than one, and one less than three."

Until that moment, Beverly hadn't

known she was capable of feeling sorry for someone and annoyed with them at the same time. "How do they compare with this place?"

"They're much better. That's what we've been told," Janet said.

"That's not good."

Janet looked around the house. "And we've got no money to fix this place. They're doing well and we aren't."

"How well are they doing exactly."

Janet shrugged her shoulders. "I don't know, but better than us I'd reckon."

"Have you approached the bank?"

"For a loan?"

Beverly nodded.

"Jeremiah won't hear of it." Janet's thin lips turned down at the corners. "Why would anyone stay here, when the other places are better?"

"That's what we've got to figure out. Either we have to make this place just as good, or we need to give people some other reason to stay here."

"Jeremiah wanted me to show you the rooms."

"Okay."

She followed Janet and was shown two large en-suited bedrooms downstairs, and the two upstairs. Altogether there were four bedrooms upstairs. Jeremiah and Janet were occupying one and Beverly was in the other one. Their rooms both had private bathrooms as well. There was also a family apartment attached to the house. It had three large bedrooms and two bathrooms, and enough sleeping space for as many as eight people.

After having looked through all the bedrooms and the apartment, Beverly saw that the only changes since she'd left had been bad ones. The Amish quilts that had once adorned the beds had been replaced with drab chenille bedspreads in depressing shades. The furniture had been downgraded too, going from functional and attractive traditional Amish pieces to garden-variety box-store units.

When they sat down in the kitchen again, Janet asked, "What do you think? You were very quiet just now."

"Where have the Amish quilts gone?"

"We sold them, and got quite a bit of money even though they were used."

"What was the point of selling them? They're going to cost a lot to replace."

"Replace?"

"Yes. The rooms aren't the same without them. And quite truthfully, the rooms are dull and uninspiring."

"They're only bedrooms—just a place to sleep."

"When people go on vacation they want somewhere nice to stay. Appealing to the eye. Somewhere homey."

"This place is homey. It's our home."

Beverly sighed.

Janet said, "There's not much point looking at the books, there's not much to see."

"When are the next guests coming?"

Janet's lips pressed together in a thin white line. "We don't have any guests booked for three whole weeks."

That is not good, Beverly thought, but she'd learned one lesson over the past months, and that was to choose to look on the bright side of things. She kept her thought to herself, and said, "That's good."

"Is it?" Janet said, wide-eyed with surprise.

"Yes. It'll give us time to whip this place into shape."

"That sounds expensive. What do you have in mind?"

"New curtains, new quilts, maybe some fresh paint. That kind of thing. I'll make a list. And I noticed you don't have a website."

"We can't do that." Janet shook her head.

"You don't need to spend a lot of money, Janet, but it does need to be functional and you need to join up with those booking websites. That's where most people book their vacations these days. I think that's why you're falling behind."

"We can't do that. It's out of the question."

"Why?"

"We can't have a computer in the place, or electricity. You know that."

"Surely the bishop would allow it for a business. I see plenty of Amish businesses that have websites."

Janet shook her head. "The bishop won't allow it."

"Some bishops allow it—they must be doing so. Just look at all the Amish who are selling things online or that have websites, both in Ohio and in Lancaster County. I'd reckon most medium sized and large Amish businesses have websites."

"It's out of the question."

Beverly groaned.

"Is there anything else you can think of?" Janet asked.

"Just fixing up the rooms and maybe interacting more with the local tourist community. These are just basic things. You probably can't see that because you're too busy trying to keep the place afloat. It takes an outsider to come in with fresh eyes to see where things can be improved."

"I don't know that I'm good at keeping the books. Are you good at that kind of thing?"

"Yes. That's my specialty at work."

"Maybe you can help me. I had someone show me, and I could do it while he was here but now I can't remember much of what he said."

"I'll take a look at what you've done. Oftentimes it's just practice." This was the first time that Janet had ever asked for her help with anything.

"I haven't done too bad a job. I've kept records of our expenditures and the money coming in. The problem is the money."

It wasn't good that Janet was admitting now she wasn't good at keeping the books. She'd been doing it for years, ever since they began the business. "I'll have a talk with *Dat*. I'll also have to take a look at those other bed-and-breakfasts. Are they run by Amish people?"

"*Nee.*"

"There you go, you have an advantage already. Here, people can experience traditional Amish food in a traditional Amish house."

"This house isn't traditional. It's been added on to too many times. Only the suite is the original house."

"I know, but it's an old Amish farmhouse all the same. The extensions were built over thirty years ago when *Mamm* and *Dat* arrived here from Lancaster County."

"It's old, I'll give it that."

Beverly chuckled.

"I'll show you where the books are kept." Janet led her to the office and reception area at the front of the house. When Beverly sat down and started leafing through the books, Janet said, "I've got things to do. I can't stand around talking all day."

Beverly looked up. "Is there anything I can help you with?"

Janet stopped walking and turned around. "You go upstairs and unpack, and the evening meal will be ready in an hour."

"Can I help you with the cooking?"

"Not unless you've improved since you left."

Beverly stood up, choosing not to react to that comment and realizing it was no good looking at messy figures when she was tired. "I'll go unpack then, and I'll go through these books tomorrow when I'm fresh."

"Just as I thought," Janet said.

Beverly walked up the stairs, wondering exactly what it was that her stepmother thought.

CHAPTER 3

BEVERLY OPENED the door of her old bedroom and pushed her suitcase out of the way with her foot, bending down to grab her handbag. She looked around the room. It was gloomy and not at all like the room she remembered from her childhood. No wonder no one wanted to stay there. When her mother was alive the home had been a happy one, now it was a dark depressing pit. Janet was the local bishop's cousin and she and Jeremiah had met at a wedding. As far as Beverly was concerned, it wasn't a great love match. No one could ever replace *Mamm* in *Dat's* heart, but she was certain Janet was in love with her father.

She put her purse on the chest of drawers, pulled her heavy suitcase across the room and lifted it onto the bed. She unzipped it and began unpacking the few things she'd brought with her. Halfway through, Beverly walked to the window and looked out at the glorious shades of green in the fields and trees below. From her window, she could see the distant rolling hills welcoming the luminous orange sun to its rest.

Her mind continued to churn as she went back to her suitcase. How was she going to look over the competing businesses? She couldn't knock on their doors and pretend she was thinking about staying there and ask to look over the rooms. It would be dishonest and, with her upbringing, she had never been comfortable with dishonesty. Besides, they might find out she was Jeremiah's daughter. She could drive past and have a good look at them. That's what she'd do, and then view their rooms on their websites. Before she'd left home, she'd had a little peek at the area's accommodation. Having no website put *Dat* and Janet's place at a significant disadvantage, and that was something she didn't think she'd be able to change. Janet was most likely right. Their community was a conservative one, and that was why it surprised Beverly that Jeremiah and Janet had welcomed her back into their home since she was officially an 'outsider.'

Beverly was already dreading the evening meal. With her father confined to his bed, she would have to sit alone and eat with Janet. And that was only if Janet decided she was willing to eat with an *Englischer.*

Just as she was putting another handful of her clothes into a drawer, she heard a car. She wandered over to the window. A middle-aged woman was getting out of a white car.

"That has to be the physical therapist," Beverly muttered to herself. She hurried down the stairs to meet her, determined to learn about the true state of her father's health.

Janet had beaten her to the front door. Standing in the doorway, the therapist smiled at Janet and then looked over her shoulder at Beverly.

Beverly stepped forward. "Hello, I'm Jeremiah's daughter."

"It's nice to meet you. I've heard all about you."

"Beverly, this is Mrs. Wilson."

The therapist put her hand out and Beverly shook it. "How's he doing?" Beverly asked.

"He's been progressing, although you might have to encourage him to do his exercises more often."

Beverly nodded. "Yes, we've already discussed that."

"I'll take you upstairs," Janet said to Mrs. Wilson as she moved swiftly past Beverly. Beverly followed them upstairs, intent on resume her unpacking. When they got to the top of the stairs, Janet turned around to face Beverly. "If you come too, that'll be too many in the room, Beverly."

"I was just off to finished my unpacking."

Janet nodded and hurried to catch up to the therapist who was walking into Jeremiah's room.

Once Beverly had unpacked everything, she heaved the empty suitcase onto the top of the freestanding wardrobe. Placing her hands on her hips, she looked around her former room and sighed. "It's going to be a long four weeks." She left her room and walked down to the kitchen to see how she could help with the evening meal.

Three quarters of an hour later, Janet and

the therapist walked down the stairs. Feeling she would be in the way, Beverly stayed in the kitchen until she heard the car drive away.

"Did everything go all right?" Beverly asked Janet when she finally came into the kitchen.

"Everything was fine. Just like always. He's getting better, but a bit slower than I'd like."

"That's good, I mean it's good that he's improving. I've peeled some vegetables for dinner."

Beverly stared at her. "Why would you do that?"

"To help out."

"But you don't know what I had planned for dinner."

"No, but, it's getting late and vegetables go with everything, don't they?"

"We're having bologna. It's already prepared as is everything else. It just needs heating."

"Well, we've got peeled vegetables ready for tomorrow night then."

"*Denke.* I appreciate you trying to help."

A backhanded compliment if ever Beverly had heard one. "You're welcome."

"Did you unpack already?"

"Yes. I didn't bring that much with me."

"Why? Aren't you going to stay the full four weeks?"

"I am, but I like to travel light."

"I hope you don't think you're going to be using the washing machine every day."

Beverly remembered the old gas-powered washing machine and hoped that they'd updated it at some point in the past ten years. "If it bothers you that much, I'll go buy more clothes if I need them."

Janet's face twisted as though she'd tasted a sour lemon. "That's wasteful."

"While we're on the subject of washing, what about *Dat's* bed sheets?"

"I do them once a week. Last wash day it was raining heavily."

"Don't you have a dryer?"

"*Nee.* In the winter, I do what we used to do and that's string things up by the fire in the kitchen. In the warmer weather if it's raining, I have Jeremiah string up a line undercover in the barn, but of course he couldn't do that now with his leg problem."

Guilt over being mean to Janet weighed heavily on her shoulders. "I'm sorry for what I said before about the sheets."

"Don't say sorry to me, say it to your *vadder.* He never liked us fighting. Did you see his face when you mentioned the sheets?"

Beverly hung her head. She'd been selfish to verbally attack Janet in the way that she had. She was an adult now, so she had to show some form of self-control. It wasn't as easy as she had thought it was going to be.

The oppressive environment brought out the worst in her. "I'll apologize to him."

"As you should."

"Let's try to get along while I'm here, okay?"

"That sounds like a good idea. *Denke* for peeling the vegetables, that was kind."

That was the nicest thing that Janet had ever said to her. The woman was truly making an effort. Beverly was so shocked all she could do was give her a smile and a little nod.

"Have you had a chance to look at our income?" Janet asked.

"No, I'll do that now, if there's time."

"You've got fifteen minutes before dinner."

Beverly left Janet and pulled out the ledgers and then sat down at the desk in the reception area. She soon realized that she'd have to put the profits and losses into spreadsheets so she could figure out where they were at. After dinner, she'd fetch her laptop from upstairs. From what she knew after several minutes, Jeremiah and Janet were beyond broke. They hadn't been able to pay their previous month's utility bills. Their only options were either to sell up now and buy a smaller place for the two of them, or to make the place work. Beverly only hoped they hadn't already borrowed against the house. She'd been told they still owned the house outright, and she hadn't come across any evidence of loan repayments.

She found Janet in the kitchen. "I've had a look at the figures."

"That was quick."

"Is there a loan against this place?"

Janet's jaw dropped. "A loan? Jeremiah is against borrowing."

"So, that's a no?"

"*Jah.*"

"Why don't you two sell this place and buy something smaller. You'll have money left over and you can invest it. You'd have an easier life."

"We've put too much into it. It was a good business in its time." She shook her head. "I don't want to sell."

Somehow it pleased Beverly that Janet was attached to the house, because she knew her father was, too. "Your financial situation isn't good."

"*Jah*, that's why your *vadder* insisted on calling you."

"I think the only way out is to get a loan, pay off what you owe and fix this place up. Then we throw a relaunch party, and get it onto the booking websites."

"That all sounds good, apart from the part about getting a loan from the bank and I'm not sure about the thing about the websites. Can you help us with the rest?"

Beverly pulled a face trying to figure out what was left of her recommendations after removing all the things Janet didn't like. "I don't see any way around getting a loan if you want to keep the place."

"You'll have to talk to Jeremiah about it."

"I'll do that tomorrow morning when he's fresh."

CHAPTER 4

BEVERLY HAD a feeling that the evening meal alone with Janet was going to be an awkward one, in spite of their earlier conversation. Everything was always that way for her when she was around her stepmother.

When the meal was heated, Beverly figured she'd do her best to put their horrible past behind her and be as helpful as she could. "Would you like me to carry *Dat's* dinner up to him?"

"I can do it."

"I know, but you must be tired of going

up and down the stairs to bring him food and everything every day. Allow me to do it."

"I've never been one to worry about hard work."

"I know, I was just trying to give you a rest that's all. We can share looking after him."

"Nee! He's my husband and I will look after him." And that was the end of it, in Janet's opinion.

"Can I do anything down here?"

"Nee. Just sit there and I'll be back in one moment. Can you do that?"

"I'll try."

Beverly had always had trouble sitting still. She was constantly fidgeting as a child, and now that she'd grown up she was no different. Her fingers drummed on the white cloth that covered the kitchen table. Her job kept her busy; it was always on her mind. It wasn't easy to come back to the slow-moving

Amish community and do nothing. There was no music like she always had at home, and playing in her earphones as she walked to work. The silence was deafening. But having no music was the least of her problems.

Janet wasn't 'one moment' like she'd said, she was gone for about ten minutes.

She rushed back into the kitchen. "There, you survived sitting quietly. That wasn't hard, was it?"

"I guess not."

There was something about being back in the kitchen with Janet that made her feel like a child again. She'd made the right decision to leave. There was no way she could have stayed in that house with Janet telling her what to do, how to act and what to say.

"How was *Dat?*

"Tired from his exercises that's what. He doesn't like to do them."

"Nobody likes to do exercises. Well, I suppose there are some people who like exercise but there wouldn't be too many."

"What are you going on about now?"

Her brain had gone numb and she found it hard to gather her thoughts. "Nothing."

"It must be something."

"I was just saying that not many people like exercising."

Janet made a noise from the back of her throat, lifted up her chin and then placed a plate of food in front of Beverly before she sat down with a plate for herself. "I suppose you don't give thanks for your food any longer?"

"Sometimes I do, but sometimes I forget." Just because she was no longer in the Amish community didn't mean that she didn't believe in God. She did, in her own way. Mainly, she was disillusioned.

"Well if you can stop talking for a few moments, I will say my own thanks to *Gott*

JEREMIAH'S DAUGHTER (AMISH ROMANCE)

for the food and you can do whatever you like."

Beverly glared at her. "Fine."

They both closed their eyes and said their silent prayers of thanks.

As she prayed, she once again reminded herself she'd have to try to be more patient while she was there. Janet was getting on in years and so was Jeremiah. She had to be calm and not react when Janet pushed her buttons or made derogatory remarks.

When they had finished the last of the meal and were stacking the dishes at the side of the sink, they both heard the unmistakable sounds of buggy wheels rolling over the gravel drive, and the clip-clopping of a horse's hooves.

"I wonder who that could be," Janet said, hurrying to the other room.

Curiosity got the better of Beverly and she was close behind Janet when she, too, looked out the living room window.

"It's my cousin, the bishop," said Janet.

Bishop Eli had always been nice to Beverly and she hoped he would be all right with her being there. Having never been baptized into the community, she'd never officially joined, so she couldn't be shunned, but she could be shut out and ignored. If the bishop didn't approve of her being there, Jeremiah and Janet would have no choice but to ask her to leave.

Janet swung the door open while Beverly headed back into the kitchen to tidy things up. It wasn't long before Janet brought the bishop back into the kitchen to greet her.

"Hello, Beverly. It's been a long time."

The bishop's kind expression told her that she wouldn't be sent on her way. "Hello, Bishop Eli. It's been ten years."

"That long? Where does the time go?"

Beverly immediately relaxed. "I don't know. I keep asking myself that. Not much has changed around here, though."

"Except that we're all older."

"Do you have good news for me?" Janet asked cutting across their conversation.

"I do. David Hilty has agreed to help you out." He turned to Beverly, and explained, "He's a carpenter."

"And he's coming here?" Beverly asked.

"That's right," Janet said with a self-satisfied grin.

"That's marvellous. *Wunderbaar,*" Beverly said.

Janet set her beady eyes on her. "You don't mind?"

"No, why would I?"

"And that's exactly what I told Jeremiah. I told him you'd would be okay with some extra people to help."

Beverly had no idea why either of them would think she'd mind someone helping with odd jobs.

"It's good to see you again, Beverly."

"And you." Beverly smiled at Eli. She'd always liked the kindly bishop, even though he had the misfortune of being related to Janet.

Janet saw the bishop out and when she came back, she said to Beverly, "He'll be here tomorrow."

"David will?" Beverly asked, wondering to whom she was referring.

"*Jah.*"

"That's good." It was the most excited she'd ever seen Janet.

Janet's gaze turned up to the ceiling. "I must tell Jeremiah. He's having a nap right now. He always sleeps after his visit from the therapist."

Beverly busied herself helping with the dishes.

WHEN BEVERLY WAS ready for bed, she said goodnight to Janet, who was knitting in the living room, and then headed up the stairs to say goodnight to her father. She pushed the door open and saw him asleep with his mouth wide open. She giggled quietly and closed the door.

It had been a long and tiring day for Beverly and she was more than ready for bed. A part of her felt a sense of security being back in her old bedroom and being amongst the Amish she'd been driven away from.

After a shower, she changed into her comfortable flannelette pajamas and slipped between the cool sheets. It wasn't long before she was fast asleep.

CHAPTER 5

BEVERLY WAS AWAKENED by the loud crowing of a rooster. It took a few seconds to realize where she was. Instead of a sparsely furnished apartment, she was faced with a white dresser that was falling apart down one side and leaning against a wall of flaking paint. At least with the bed-and-breakfast things to occupy her mind, she wouldn't think about Kevin, her ex, and spend hours wondering why he suddenly dropped her to marry his former girlfriend.

After taking a few moments to gather her

thoughts, she sat up and stretched her arms over her head. If she could borrow a buggy, she'd drive past the two bed-and-breakfasts that Janet had mentioned. She'd also have to do those spreadsheets before her computer lost all its charge. Maybe she could find time to take it into town to recharge at a café or a coffee shop.

The clock on the nightstand told her it was already past seven. That meant Janet had been awake for hours. Janet used to be an early riser and Beverly doubted that she'd changed her habits.

She readied herself for the day, choosing a dress rather than wearing pants like she'd arrived in, and headed down to the kitchen.

Just as she'd suspected, Janet was bustling around making breakfast. The mingled aromas of bacon and eggs and freshly ground coffee filled the air.

Janet looked her up and down. "Ah, that's

an improvement and just in time too. Can I cook you some eggs?"

"Yes please."

"I'll just take this up to Jeremiah." She set a plate of bacon, eggs and toast on a tray, and added a mug of coffee.

"Do you want me to take that up?" Beverly offered.

"No, that's all right. I'll do it."

Beverly knew that was going to be Janet's response but still felt she should make the offer. She poured herself a cup of coffee from the pot and sat down at the kitchen table. It was odd being there without guests around the table. The place had been a guest house for so long that she was used to sharing the kitchen table and eating to the buzz of many conversations as Janet cooked everyone a hearty breakfast.

When Janet finally came back down the stairs, Beverly asked if she could borrow the buggy.

"That's fine," Janet said. "We only have one horse these days and that's Trevor."

"Trevor?" Beverly giggled, wondering if she'd heard right.

Janet's lips twitched with amusement. "It's not our fault. The previous owners named him that."

"It's an unusual name for a horse."

Janet chuckled. "It is. How would you like your eggs?"

"It doesn't matter to me."

Janet stared at her. "It's easier if you just tell me."

"Just scrambled, thanks."

"I see you've already helped yourself to the coffee. Yuck; I also see you're having it black."

"Yes."

She stopped still and continued to stare. "You never used to drink it."

"I was too young when I left, but I like it

now. As soon as I wake, I look forward to having a cup. The stronger, the better."

"You take after your *vadder* with coffee. He likes his black, too, and I can't stand the stuff. I do like the smell of it, but that's about all. I much prefer hot tea."

It pleased Beverly that Janet was being chatty; it was a good sign, indicating her stepmother was making an effort. If Janet was prepared to make an effort, then she would too.

"David's arriving today."

"Yes, I know. That's good."

"I'm putting him in the suite since we don't have any bookings for it."

Beverly knew her reasoning. Janet didn't want to have two single people under the same roof and they wouldn't be if David stayed in the suite because that was attached but still separate from the main house. It wouldn't have occurred to Janet that the bed-

and-breakfast wasn't the same as a normal house. She'd always been a stickler for the rules even in cases where they made no sense. *How would Janet have handled unmarried couples staying as guests?* Beverly wondered.

Janet placed a plate of food in front of Beverly.

"Thank you," Beverly said.

"You're welcome."

She looked over at Janet. "Are you having any?"

"I've already had mine. I wake up very early in the morning."

"I remember that you always woke early. Nothing's changed then."

"I like to watch the sun rise. It's the best time of the day, especially in the summer months."

"I can't remember the last time I watched the sun come up. I sleep too late. How's *Dat* this morning?"

"About the same. He'll improve. He's a very determined man."

"I know."

"He never had a day's sickness in his life," Janet added.

Beverly nodded. "As far back as I can remember he never had so much as a cold."

"That's right. He's got a strong constitution."

Janet sat down with her delicate china cup filled with hot tea, and Beverly wondered if Janet was ever sad about not having any children of her own. She wasn't brave enough to ask just in case she told her that she was the cause—that Beverly was so awful that she'd turned her off having children altogether. Then Beverly did the math. Janet would've been too old by the time she had married Beverly's father to have had any. The two of them sat there for moments in awkward silence.

Beverly pushed her hair away from her

face. It was so straight it always fell over her face unless she tied it back. For work she always pinned it up. "It seems like it's going to be a nice day."

"I hope so, because today's washing day."

"Look, I'm so sorry what I said before about the sheets. I just get angry sometimes and things come out of my mouth without me thinking."

"It doesn't bother me. Anyway, you've already apologized about that. Don't you remember? If you don't remember it can't have been a genuine apology."

"It was genuine. I was exhausted last night. The bus trip was tiring. It was a genuine apology, then and now, both of them."

"Then I accept it—both of them."

Janet drank the last of her tea while Beverly finished breakfast and then went upstairs to fetch the dishes from her father. Jeremiah was dozing, so she quietly collected the tray and took it back to the kitchen. "Do you want me to help you with that?" she asked Janet, referring to the dishes.

"Okay, if you help me with this, I'll help you hitch the buggy. What time were you thinking of leaving?"

"Sometime this morning I guess. I've already looked at the two competitors online before I got here—their rooms—and I'll drive past the buildings to see what the grounds are like."

"Very good. What about the rooms?"

"I looked at their photos on the Internet," Beverly explained again.

"It would be different being there in real life and taking a look around."

Beverly shook her head. "I don't think that's going to happen, is it? Wouldn't it be weird if we asked to look around?"

"*Jah,* it would. I wouldn't like to ask. Want to go when we finish this washing up?"

"Okay, but what about David?"

"We'll leave the door open. He can come in and get himself settled."

"He's been here before?"

"*Nee.*"

"Oh. Should we leave *Dat* here by himself?"

"We won't be that long. It's not far away."

Beverly looked down at her flip-flops. "I'll need to put shoes on."

Janet went to catch the horse from his small paddock while Beverly went to her room to change her shoes.

"That must be David now," Beverly said to herself. She'd lived alone for so long she was used to talking to herself. It was nothing unusual. When she looked out the window, she watched Janet walk to a car. It wasn't a taxi. By the time she got downstairs and opened the front door, she saw an *Englischer* talking to Janet, not an Amish man like she'd been expecting. Naturally, she hoped it was a guest who wanted to stay there. Looking closer, it appeared the man was telling Janet something rather than asking about a room. Beverly wasted no time going down the stairs and outside, hurrying over to hear what was being said.

CHAPTER 6

"Hello," Beverly said when she was only feet away from the two of them.

Janet turned around. "Beverly, this man says he wants to buy our *haus.*"

"Oh." Beverly wondered if this was God's way out for Jeremiah and Janet. It would also relieve her of a lot of stress and hard work, which sounded good to her. "Really?" As she studied him closer, though, she didn't think he looked at all the type who'd want to buy a place like theirs.

He was reasonably handsome, looked to

be in his late thirties, and, going by his late-model Mercedes, she figured he wasn't short of a dollar. "Were you interested in the place as an ongoing business?"

"Beverly, it's not for sale. I was just telling Mr. ..."

"Reynolds." He stepped forward and shook Beverly's hand. "Oscar Reynolds."

Beverly smiled. "Hello, Oscar. I'm Beverly Beiler."

He gave a quick nod. "I'm interested in the house, and truthfully, I'm not certain what I'll use it for yet. Initially, it'll be a getaway for me. Somewhere ... let's say, a weekender, a vacation house."

That confirmed to Beverly that he was wealthy, if he wanted their huge home as a weekend getaway place.

"Why are you so interested? Do you mind if I ask?" Janet usually hid her obnoxious personality from strangers, but this time it was coming through loud and clear and in bucket loads. It wasn't what Janet said, but the way she said it.

A slight grin appeared around the corners of his mouth when he looked back up at the house. "I used to go past it when I was a kid and I wondered what it would be like to live here. I've always admired this place."

Beverly wasn't really listening to his words; she was lost in his clear blue eyes, several shades darker than her own. They stood out nicely against his honey-colored smooth skin. "You're from around here then?" she asked.

He fixed his eyes on Beverly. "I grew up not far away, and then I moved away for college. I want to move back one day—at some point in the future. I'm living in New York City right now."

"That's where I'm from."

"Really? You live there?"

Beverly looked at his left hand to see if he

was wearing a ring and was pleased he wasn't. "Yes."

"Are you Janet's daughter?"

"I'm her stepdaughter. I used to live here and then I moved to the city and I'm working in banking. I'm a regional loans manager." She hoped she wasn't telling him too much, but she was excited to meet a man like him and especially pleased that he'd grown up in the valley close to her child-hood home. Having a similar background was a good start to any relationship. In that moment, the fact that he was raised *Englisch* and she Amish didn't occur to her.

"I work for a law firm."

"You're a lawyer?"

"Yes."

When they talked further, Beverly dis-covered they worked about five hundred yards from each other on the same street in the financial district. And lived within blocks of each other.

Oscar looked back over at Janet, who was glaring at the two of them. "I can pay a good price. Don't worry, I'm not here to steal the place."

"We could at least hear him out, Janet."

"It's not for sale," she snapped with all the menace of a deadly venomous snake.

"Well, it might be in the future." Beverly was doing her best to be polite to make up for Janet.

"*Jah,* when we're dead and gone," Janet said, now showing the depths of her true personality.

A nervous giggle escaped Beverly's lips. If this man was willing to pay them a good figure, she didn't want him to be offended by Janet. He might be the very answer—the very thing they needed to pull them out of the financial hole.

"I'll give you my card." Oscar reached into his pocket and pulled out a business card and handed it to Beverly. "How long are you here for, Beverly?"

"A couple more weeks." She stared at the white glossy card with its gold writing, and then looked back up at him.

"I'm here for a week," he said, "maybe more. Perhaps the two of us could talk a little more about this over a drink?"

She was flattered. It was so hard to meet good men in the city and something told Beverly that he was a good one. If only Janet wasn't staring at her, waiting to hear what the next words out of her mouth would be. Beverly glanced at Janet's disapproving face and was determined not to let her step-mother stand in her way. She smiled at Oscar. "I'd like that."

Janet pushed out her lower jaw. "You can't go anywhere. You'll be too busy here."

"I'm sure I can spare a little time to have a quick coffee to hear more of what Mr. Reynolds has to say. Before I do, you might be able to discuss the possibility of selling the place with *Dat*."

"Please, it's Oscar. How about later this afternoon?" Oscar asked Beverly.

Janet snapped. "No! We've got a visitor arriving today."

He hadn't taken his eyes from Beverly. "Why don't we make it tomorrow afternoon? If you're free?"

"Perfect."

He grinned at Beverly showing his evenly-shaped white teeth. "Why don't I collect you around four?"

Beverly smiled. "Okay." She could feel Janet's beady eyes boring right through her, but she didn't care. He was perfect. Oscar had a good job and he'd grown up right by her and loved the house she grew up in. Allowing her mind to drift to a happy place, she imagined they would get married, live in a city apartment and come to the homestead for vacations and weekends. Maybe, Janet and Jeremiah could stay on and live there, since there was plenty of room.

"I don't think we'll sell," Janet told him.

"If you change your mind I'll make you a good offer. One you can't refuse."

Janet's face brightened at that. "I'll talk to my husband."

After Oscar gave Janet a huge smile, he gave Beverly a nod and slid back into the driver's seat of his sleek car. Beverly and Janet watched him turn the steel-gray Mercedes and they listened to it purr down the driveway.

"What do you think of that, Janet? It's an answer to prayer. He said he'll offer a good price and he won't care about the takings being low. Anyone else would, I'm guessing."

"Then where would we live?" Janet asked.

"You could buy something much smaller and have a simpler, easier life. How does that sound?"

"But where?"

"I don't know. You'll find something. Don't you think it's an answer to prayer?" Beverly was certainly thinking this man was an answer to hers.

"It sounds okay, I suppose. It depends how good his offer is and if we can find another place to live."

"I'll try to find out how much he's thinking tomorrow afternoon."

Janet stared at her with her dark eyes now bulging. "You were throwing yourself at him."

"I was not." If she had been, he didn't seem to mind.

"You were. A man won't respect you if you act like that."

Beverly thought back to what she'd done and said; she didn't think she was being obvious. All she'd done was accept his invitation. Movement from the road caught Beverly's eye. It was a taxi. "Janet, this might be your cousin."

Janet looked over. "You mean my nephew."

"Yes, sorry, your nephew."

They watched the taxi pull up, and a tall Amish man got out.

CHAPTER 7

He flashed a smile at them and went behind the taxi to fetch his suitcase out of the trunk. Janet hurried over to him, reached up on her tiptoes, and he had to bend down so she could kiss him on his cheek. Janet said something and then he looked over at Beverly. Janet must've explained who she was.

He picked up the suitcase and both he and Janet walked toward her.

Janet introduced them. "David, this is Jeremiah's daughter, Beverly."

"Hello. It's nice to meet you."

She reached out her hand and he shook it. "Hello." He didn't seem so bad for a relative of Janet's.

"This is David, my nephew all the way from Walnut Creek. I haven't seen him since he was a little *bu*."

David gave an embarrassed chuckle.

"You've grown into a man," Janet said.

"Time will do that to a boy."

"Walnut Creek?" Beverly asked.

"Ohio," David said.

Janet stared at Beverly. "You don't have to do that thing you were going to do today, do you?"

"The thing I was going to do this morning?"

"*Jah*. I'm not talking about the thing you're doing tomorrow afternoon."

Beverly understood she was talking about driving past the bed-and-breakfasts, but why the need for secrecy? "No, I don't have to do it today, but I wanted to."

JEREMIAH'S DAUGHTER (AMISH ROMANCE)

They walked up the stairs of the porch.

Janet sighed as she pushed the front door open. "I suppose the sooner you do things like that, the better it will be. Perhaps you can take David with you."

"Where are we going?" David asked, raising his eyebrows and tilting his head questioningly.

"I was going to drive past the other bed-and-breakfast spots in the area. I believe there are two that have recently opened; I don't think you'd be interested in that."

The sound of Jeremiah's brass bell rang through the air and a flustered-looking Janet hurried up the stairs to see what he wanted, leaving David and Beverly just inside the door on their own.

"It makes sense that I'd go with you. I was asked to come here to see how I could improve things."

"Oh? I thought you were coming here to

do odd jobs and what not. Aren't you a carpenter?"

"*Nee.*"

"Janet told me you were a carpenter."

He chuckled. "I don't know why she thinks that. I can do all those sorts of things, but I'm not a professional. Bishop Eli sent a letter to one of my brothers asking if he knew anyone who might be able to help improve the occupancy rates. I volunteered my services."

Most Amish men could build things the same as most Amish women could cook and sew. It was unusual if they couldn't.

He glanced down at her clothes. "Are you on vacation?"

Beverly shrugged. "They also wanted me to help with improving things."

"That's funny, that's why they called me."

Beverly pressed her lips together. This must've been all Janet's doing. "If I had known they had someone else coming, I

JEREMIAH'S DAUGHTER (AMISH ROMANCE)

don't know if I would've come back here."
She stared at him to let him know she was
annoyed her time was being wasted. "And
what experience have you had?" she asked
after she'd decided it surely wasn't his fault.

"My *bruder,* Thomas, runs a very successful bed-and-breakfast in Ohio and I've
helped him quite a bit."

"Oh, then I needn't have come here," Beverly mumbled.

"Where are you from?"

"New York city."

"And you're Jeremiah's *dochder?*"

"That's right. Janet has never mentioned
me?"

"We're not that close. There are dozens of
cousins in my family and just as many aunts
and *onkels.* Both my parents come from families of twelve."

"There's only me in my family."

"You have no sisters or brothers?"

"No. It was just me."

"It must've been lonely growing up."

"I never thought so. I had the baby animals. We had a little farm here, so there were plenty of animals, and I had lots of friends."

He chuckled. "That's one thing about growing up in a large Amish community there are always plenty of children."

"Do you have any inspirations at the moment? What are your first impressions?"

He looked around. "It might need a lick of paint."

"I could go home now that you're here to take over." She hadn't meant what she said to sound rude, but in her experience too many people doing the same job was counterproductive. She had a flash of insight. That had been Janet's point about the cooking yesterday.

"I think they'll need both of us. I think we'll make a good team."

She looked at his smiling face. Maybe there was a reason God had brought her back. Here was the second man she'd found herself attracted to and she hadn't even been there twenty-four hours. She hoped it wasn't some kind of test from God on whether she would choose an *Englischer* or an Amish man. "You seriously think we'll make a good team?"

"*Jah.* I'm sure of it."

Beverly leaned in, and whispered, "They've run out of money to do improvements. They'd have to borrow."

"You'll have to convince Jeremiah to borrow the money from somewhere," he said.

"That's the first hurdle, but then there's the question of whether the bank will lend them the money. And if the bankers think they can't meet the repayments, they won't get the loan. This place is the only income they've got. We'll need to put a proposal together to present to the bank, with some projected figures—"

"That's where you come in. I can't help you there. Janet told me you work in a bank."

"She did?" That must've been what she whispered to him when he arrived.

"Jah."

"That's right. I'm a loans manager, funnily enough."

"Good, you should have some contacts in the bank."

"What do you mean?"

"It helps to know people. Maybe you could persuade them to give them money."

"Maybe yes, maybe no, we'll see. If the numbers don't stack up he won't get the loan no matter what contacts I've got. We've got loan approval guidelines we need to follow."

"I'm sure you can pull some strings."

She puffed out a breath of air. "We'll have to figure out what we're going to do before we can know what everything is going to cost."

"Okay, shall we do that today?"

"Okay. Sure. The sooner we start, the sooner we can draft that proposal."

Janet came back down the stairs. "Show David to the suite would you, Beverly?"

"All right. Is *Dat* okay?"

"*Jah,* he just wanted a cup of hot tea." Janet bustled past them.

"This way. It's back outside," Beverly said to David as he followed her outside. "The suite, as Janet calls it, was originally the old homestead. It gets freezing there in winter. It has the original oak floorboards and the foundations are stone, so the biting cold wind comes up through the floorboards." She flung the door open.

He stepped through and looked around. "Nice."

"You like it?"

"I do. It looks lovely."

"It does, I agree, but wait until you see the rooms in the house. They aren't very good." Beverly looked around the living room of the suite. "This room's not so bad. Anyway, why don't you unpack and get settled, and then meet me back in the main house? We'll go room to room and make a list of what needs to be done."

"Okay." He smiled.

"What's funny?"

"I'm not used to being ordered about."

"Oh." Beverly giggled. "I'm sorry. I'm used to organizing myself and my assistants."

"I don't mind. I'll come and find you as soon as I poke my head in and say hello to Jeremiah."

"Good. I'll see you soon." Beverly walked out and closed the door behind her. She puffed out a huge breath. "Why?" she asked in a whisper as she looked up to the sky, not believing she'd met two good men. Both of the men she'd met today had made her heart race, something that hadn't happened in a long time.

CHAPTER 8

LATER, with pen and paper in hand, Beverly and David went from room to room discussing what needed to be done and estimating the costs.

"We've got six guest rooms, each with a private bathroom. Then we've got the suite where you're staying, which sleeps six to eight. It's very popular with families, or it used to be, back when I was living here."

"Did you resent people being in your home?"

"No. I enjoyed helping Janet, and the guests were always so lovely to me."

"You've got the personality to run a place like this."

"Thank you, I think."

He chuckled. "It was a compliment."

"I was hoping so. Anyway... There's the room that Jeremiah and Janet occupy; we can't count that one, so that leaves five guest rooms with private baths."

"We're not updating their room?"

"Of course not. They're happy with it the way it is."

"Aha."

"We'll start in the room I'm staying in." She swung the door open, pleased that she had left it tidy.

"This is your bedroom from when you were a child?"

"It was. But it's changed a lot. I had a single bed instead of this double bed and I had an old-fashioned closet and now they've got this wardrobe, which I think is kind of ugly, but it's probably too expensive to replace. If we bought an old-fashioned dresser of similar style it would be better than that one." Beverly nodded to the chest of drawers that was falling apart.

"And I write that down?" He was the one with the pen and paper.

"Yes. 'One wooden chest of drawers with character.' That's what we need." She looked around the walls. "And this room needs painting and the floors are a bit scratched up. They might come up okay with a good scrubbing and waxing, and if we get a large rug I think we can get away with it."

"Clean and wax floor, large rug, and paint." he murmured as he wrote it down. He looked up. "Is that all for this room?"

"Yes." They walked into the next room. Beverly looked out the window and saw it had a good view of the road. "I've always liked this room."

"Why wasn't this your room, then?" he asked.

"I don't know. It just wasn't."

Just when she was about to say that she remembered that all the rooms needed new Amish quilts, he asked, "What are your first memories of Janet?"

She turned around and looked at him, surprised. Did he really want to know what she thought of Janet? And how should she phrase her answer? "I can't really remember. They got married pretty quickly. I hardly had time to get to know her."

"It must have been a big adjustment to make after your *mudder* died."

"They married two years, almost to the day, after she died." She turned away from him and looked out the window, over the top of the leafy trees and out to the road beyond. "They married when I was thirteen."

"You were eleven when your *mudder* died?"

"That's right, a time when a girl needs her mother. I guess at any age a girl needs her mother. Even now, but that's not meant to …" her voice trailed off.

"You've got Janet."

"Yes." She turned around and looked at him. "I've got Janet."

"And have you always gotten along with her?"

"You do ask a lot of questions."

"Forgive me, but I've always been too nosy for my own good." He chuckled. "I just noticed that there seems to be some tension."

"I'm trying to get along, put it that way, and she is too. Otherwise, she wouldn't have had me back here."

He raised his eyebrows. "Is that so?"

"I didn't leave on the best of terms with her, or *Dat*. Well, it didn't please him that I left on bad terms with her."

"Aha."

"I haven't been back in ten years. We

never really got along, Janet and I, and I'm not sure why." The woman irritated her, but she couldn't say that to David or she'd sound like a real cow. "But here I am as soon as my father called me. I came back, which means I have a sense of duty toward him. He is my father, after all."

"Did you have much contact with him while you were gone?"

"None."

"What?"

"None."

"*Jah*, I heard you, but I'm having trouble taking that in."

She was keen to get the focus off herself. "What about you? Why did you drop everything and come here?"

"I needed time by myself—time to think some things through."

"What do you do for a living?"

"I own a sawmill with one of my brothers."

"Ah, it sounds like that would keep you really busy. It was good you could get time off."

"That's one of the advantages of co-owning a business, I guess. We cover for each other when we need the time. He has nine children. Can you believe it? He's only a little older than I am."

"He must've started young."

"He did. And he's taken time off after each one was born, so he didn't hesitate to agree to me taking some time for myself."

She looked around the room once again. "I forgot to mention, all the bedrooms need new Amish quilts—proper ones. The suite where you're staying only needs a double bed quilt. The others look okay."

He wrote that down. "What else do we need in here?"

"New nightstands. I don't know where they got this particle-board furniture from.

It looks like they've been pulled out of a dumpster."

He chuckled. "I'll agree with you on that."

"I wonder what they did with all the nice furniture that used to be in here. And this room would need a new rug too. To hide all the scratches that are close to the bed." She ran the toe of her black lace-up boot over the scratches.

"Okay, new rug. Do you think a scrub-and-polish would help cover them?"

"Maybe. Probably."

He wrote everything down. Then he looked up at her. "Have you kept in contact with anyone from the community?"

She shook her head. "I do have two special friends that I grew up with. I can't wait to see them again. I'm hoping to visit with them while I'm here. They're probably both married with six children each by now. It would have felt weird to write to them when I was writing to my father and getting no replies. Do you know what I mean?"

He nodded. "Absolutely."

"We three girls were inseparable. I was closer to them because I was an only child. They were like my sisters. I missed them dreadfully."

"They must miss you too."

"I hope so. I hope they haven't forgotten me. I might show up on the doorstep and they'll say, 'Who are you?'"

He chuckled. "I don't think so. You're the kind of woman that no one would forget."

She broke into a smile, and knew there was true kindness in those words. She couldn't help smiling when she felt the butterflies in her tummy. He was a man who could very easily make her forget she'd recently been dumped by the man who had asked her to marry him. What was his name again?

When they had finished inspecting all the

rooms, it was mid-afternoon and Beverly's head was racing.

She was attracted to David, and the fact that he might have similar feelings was confirmed when he said, "Why don't we escape this place tonight?"

She tried to slow her breathing. "Escape? You've only just arrived."

"I know, but it would be nice if we could go somewhere quiet." He leaned in. "Aunt Janet makes me a little nervous. I feel like relaxing."

Beverly giggled. "I can understand that. What do you have in mind?"

"A quick dinner out, somewhere in town. It won't be a late night."

"That sounds good to me." Either he liked her, or he wasn't any keener on having a dinner with Janet than she was.

"On the condition that you tell me more about yourself," he added.

She smiled when she saw the cheeky look

on his face. "There's not much more to tell. I think I told you everything." She hadn't told him about her tragic love life, and neither would she.

"I think there's a lot more to you than you're telling me."

"Do you think Janet will be okay with us not having dinner here?"

"It'll save her cooking, won't it?"

"She likes to cook."

"Do you think it'll be a problem?"

Beverly shrugged. "Ask her and find out."

"Me?"

"Yes, you. I'm certainly not going to do it."

He smiled and shook his head at her. "I guess that leaves it up to me, then." He leaned in closer. "Do you think Janet will allow us to leave the house together?"

"We could go in separate buggies."

"That's not what I meant. Do you think she will let us leave at all?"

"I certainly hope so. Ask her. I've got a

feeling you'll have a better chance of persuading her than I would have."

He chuckled. "You might be right."

"Go on ask her. She's in the kitchen. I'll stay close by and listen at the door."

He chuckled. "Okay. I'll do my best."

She walked with him to just outside the kitchen door, stopped, and just as he got close to the door she gave him a playful push to help him inside. He glanced back at her and gave her a little frown, which made her giggle. Beverly saw that Janet was standing at the kitchen sink with her back turned, and she quickly stifled the giggle and ducked around the corner, making sure she was out of sight.

"Aunt Janet, would you mind very much if Beverly and I had dinner in town tonight?"

Beverly's pulse raced and she put her hand over her mouth to stop herself from laughing. She knew Janet wouldn't approve. David had no idea who he was up against.

"Why would you want to have dinner somewhere else?"

Beverly just knew Janet would've had her hands on her hips, feet planted firmly and her lower jaw jutting out. It was funny to hear someone else in Janet's line of fire.

David kept trying. "It's just that you've been working so hard, Aunt Janet, and we figured you might like a break from the cooking."

"So, this was Beverly's idea?"

Beverly shook her head, wondering how the blame had turned onto her.

"It definitely wasn't her idea. It was mine. I'd like to take Beverly out for a quick meal and we'll bring you and Jeremiah back some take-out. How does that sound?"

"*Nee.* I haven't been working hard at all. We haven't had any guests for the past two weeks. There will just be the four of us for dinner and that's no trouble at all."

Since David wasn't having any success,

Beverly figured she'd better help him out and she stepped in the room. "Janet, I'd like to show David the town."

"He won't be able to see anything in the dark, now, will he?"

Beverly opened her mouth and then realized she had no comeback.

"He's here for two weeks, so there's plenty of time for that." Janet spoke as though it had been decided that they weren't going anywhere. She turned back to her stove.

Beverly and David exchanged glances, both knowing it was no use. Janet wasn't budging.

"What do you say?" David asked Beverly.

"Janet has a point. I suppose there's plenty of time to see the town." Beverly had been trapped. What else could she have said?

David looked back at Janet. *"Denke.* We will both eat here tonight."

Janet gave a sharp nod. "As it should be."

"Can I do anything before dinner? Are there any odd jobs that need to be done?" he asked.

"We'll find things for you to do tomorrow. Why don't you have a rest in the living room while Beverly helps me in here?"

He gave both ladies a smile and headed out of the room, giving Beverly a look that said he knew she was left to face the dragon.

"What can I do?" Beverly asked.

Janet stepped closer to her. "I know what you're up to. You're trying to lead that boy astray."

Beverly face scrunched. "Who? David?"

"Who else would I be talking about?"

"He's hardly a boy and I'm not doing anything to him."

"I saw the way you looked at him."

Beverly opened her mouth to speak, but whatever she'd say next would only incriminate herself. She had no words. Yes, she was attracted to him, but no, she had no intention of leading anyone astray. David was old enough to make up his own mind about whatever he wanted to do.

Beverly rubbed her forehead. "What would you like me to do in here, Janet?"

"Peel the vegetables."

"Sure."

Janet wagged a finger at her. "I'll be watching you with him."

"I came back here to help make the bed-and-breakfast successful again, and that's all I'm doing here. When I leave here, I have no intention of giving myself any reason to return."

"You haven't changed a bit."

Beverly whipped her head around. "I never said I had. It appears you haven't either."

"Let's just try and get along for your *vadder's* sake."

"That's fine. In front of him, we can get along."

"Good."

"Fine," Beverly said.

"You always did want to have the last word."

"Isn't that what you were doing just now, Janet?"

"*Nee.*"

Beverly remained silent deliberately so Janet could satisfy herself with having the last word. She unfolded the old newspaper on the end of the table, took a peeler from the drawer and picked up the first of the vegetables that Janet had placed on the table. "What about the ones I peeled yesterday?"

"I forgot you did that. Hmm. That's why it's best that there's only one cook in the kitchen."

"That's fine with me." Beverly pushed out her chair and stood up. "I'll take some tea out to David."

Janet didn't say anything further while Beverly made the tea.

When she reached the living room with the hot tea, David put the Amish newspaper he was reading onto the couch beside him. *"Denke."*

Beverly sat down with him.

"Did Janet want you to help her?" he asked.

"All she'll allow me to do is peel vegetables, and I did that last night and we haven't used them yet."

"Ah." He took a sip of hot tea.

She wanted to find out more about him, but she didn't want to ask too many questions at once. "I do hope we'll be able to turn this place around."

"We'll get a better idea tomorrow when we look at those other two bed-and-breakfasts."

"Dat and Janet need a website."

"Is that really necessary?"

"Unless somebody can come up with a better idea."

"Then we must try to come up with a better idea."

Beverly sipped on her tea, wishing it were coffee. She rarely had coffee late in the afternoon because it prevented her sleeping well at night, but she was in the mood for it right now. The tea would have to do. She wasn't looking forward to dinner with Janet because she wouldn't be able to talk freely with David. Janet would be judging every movement, every facial expression and every word. Beverly wondered if David found Janet just as unpleasant.

"I should talk to *Dat* about getting a loan."

"Now?"

"Jah. Before dinner." She stood and headed up to her father.

After she knocked gently on his door she heard him tell her to come in.

"David and I have gone room by room, listing everything that we're going to need."

He ran his hand over his forehead. "And how much does it all add up to?"

"Probably about ten thousand."

"I don't have ten thousand dollars."

"I do. I could loan it to you."

"*Nee!* I won't hear of it."

"But, *Dat—*"

"It's no use. My mind's made up. I'd borrow from a bank before I'd borrow from you."

"Does that mean you will borrow from a bank?"

"*Nee.*"

Beverly sighed and looked down at the floorboards. Something had to be done; some decision had to be made. "If you don't borrow a small amount, you might have to sell the place."

His bottom lip wobbled above his long gray beard. "I've never borrowed money."

"I know, *Dat,* but you pretty much need

to. It's nothing shameful. Most people borrow money, even Amish people."

"It goes against everything I believe in."

"I don't think it does. I just think you're being stubborn."

He sighed. "I'll talk it over with Janet."

Beverly was pleased that she seemed to be making headway. "Okay."

"Is dinner coming soon?"

"*Jah,* Janet is cooking it right now."

He nestled his head back down into the pillow and he closed his eyes. "Good."

Apparently, that was the end of the conversation. "Goodnight, *Dat.*"

After he had mumbled his goodnight, Beverly left him alone.

CHAPTER 9

JANET HAD ALWAYS BEEN a marvelous cook and nothing had changed in that department. They sat down to a dinner of pork chops with mushrooms and, of course, vegetables.

"What do you have planned for tomorrow, Beverly?" Janet asked her.

"I plan to do what I was going to do today, go past the other bed-and-breakfasts."

"I offered to go with her," David said.

Janet looked at David and then looked back at Beverly and remained quiet.

"With David's experience, he'll be an asset around here," Beverly said.

"Weren't you having a drink with that Oscar fellow? Aren't you doing that tomorrow?"

Beverly nearly dropped her fork, and she quickly swallowed the bite of pork she'd just placed into her mouth. She could see that David was taken aback. "It's coffee. It's not a drink and it's just business." She looked at David and explained, "I don't know if Janet told you, but there's a lawyer from the city who's interested in buying this place."

He whipped his head around to Janet. "You didn't tell me you were even thinking of selling."

"We weren't, but it is an option if this place doesn't improve. I mean, if it doesn't improve, we might have no choice but to sell. We don't like owing money to people."

"And you're having dinner with him to negotiate a price?" David asked Beverly.

"No I'm not. We're just talking over coffee. He wanted to talk more about buying the place. I think he's going to make an offer."

"It better be a good offer," Janet snapped.

"If it's not a good offer, you don't have to take it."

"I'm well aware of how such things work, Beverly." Janet's words were snarled.

Beverly looked down at her food, and slowly cut herself another portion of meat. Why did Janet have to open her big mouth about Oscar? Having a drink with him sounded so decadent, especially the way she'd blurted it out like that, as though it was a wicked secret.

"I told Bishop Eli I would help him and some of the men tomorrow afternoon, with a barn repair. I don't have many details about it. All I know is he's coming to collect me at two in the afternoon and then bringing me back when it's finished."

"Very good," Janet said. "We must do what we can to help others."

"Shall we head off after breakfast in the morning, Beverly?" he asked. "We'll make an early start so we'll both be back in time for the other things we have to do."

She nodded. "That sounds good."

"Yeah, and then you'll be free to meet that lawyer in the evening for a drink."

"It's not a drink, Janet, not the way you're implying. The meeting is to discuss this place since you said you didn't have time to talk with him when he was here."

Janet nodded. "I suppose its best you talk to him since you're used to dealing with those kinds of people."

Beverly didn't know whether she meant that she was used to dealing with *Englischers,* or dealing with lawyers. Either way, what Janet had said didn't sound very good. She kept her head down in the hope that David didn't think less of her now.

"The food's very good, as always, Janet," Beverly said.

"It certainly is," David agreed.

Janet chortled. "I have had a lot of practice cooking. I once cooked for three hundred people on my own, can you believe that?"

"Wow, that's a lot of people. Are you sure it was that many?" Beverly asked.

Before Janet could answer, David asked, "Where was that, at a wedding?"

"It was a cousin's birthday party. I was supposed to have two other women help me, but they couldn't come at the last minute. Other women there offered to help, but I preferred to do it alone."

"That's impressive," Beverly said.

"It was help-yourself as we normally have it, but I cooked all the chickens, the roasted meats, and all the vegetables too, as well as most of the desserts."

"Sometimes we don't know what we're

capable of until we're put to the test," David said.

That reminded Beverly that God might very well be testing her right now. Testing her to finally be patient with Janet. Sometimes she could do it, and then Janet would say one more little thing and cause her to snap. Now that Janet and she had agreed to get along in front of Jeremiah, that was exactly what they had to do. And they'd best practice when away from him, too.

When they finished the last of the meal, Janet announced that there was rhubarb and apple pie warming in the oven and she would serve it with a scoop of ice cream and a dollop of cream. Beverly knew she'd gain weight over these next few weeks.

After dinner, David excused himself for an early night. Beverly insisted that Janet have a rest, and she washed up the dishes and cleaned the kitchen before she too went to bed. Being in the kitchen alone reminded her of her mother. The small oven had been replaced with a much larger one but the large stone fireplace was still there and the countertops and cupboards were still the same. Janet had taken it over many years ago, but still it was the same kitchen in which her mother had taught her to cook. Much like Janet, her mother had been an excellent cook and if she had lived longer she would've passed along her many secrets to Beverly. When her mother died, her father had taken over the cooking. In any other Amish household, the daughter would've cooked for the father even at that tender age. Beverly suspected her father felt closer to her mother when he followed those recipes from her scrapbook. Even though he carefully followed the recipes step-by-step, the food never tasted the same. Soon after Janet married her father, the scrapbook that seemed to somehow embody her mother had disappeared out of the kitchen. Beverly never asked where it went. She knew in her heart that Janet had destroyed it—most likely in a jealous rage.

THE NEXT MORNING, when Beverly walked down the stairs, she saw a familiar figure washing the floorboards in the living room. "Mrs. Stoltzfus?"

Mrs. Stoltzfus straightened up and grinned from ear-to-ear when she saw her. "Beverly! Good morning. I heard you were back." She opened her arms, inviting a hug.

Beverly stepped forward and embraced the woman lightly and then stepped back. "How have you been?"

"Nothing much has changed except Levi got married and had twins, both boys. They're two years old now."

Levi was the last of her sons to get married. He was in his late twenties when Beverly left and she remembered him as almost a tragic lonely figure. "He got married. That's fantastic."

"*Jah*, and he married one of your friends."

"One of my friends?" Beverly couldn't think who it could be.

"Betsy," Mrs. Stoltzfus said with laughter ringing in her voice.

"Betsy married Levi?"

"That's right."

"Well, I'm sure so much more has happened. Betsy was a good friend of mine, and so was Leah. I can't wait to catch up with them."

"You can see Leah because she doesn't live far from here, but Betsy and Levi moved to Ohio."

"That's sad that you don't have them living nearby."

"They visit us and they write."

"That's good. Where does Leah live? Oh, and who did she marry?"

"Leah is married to Benjamin Yoder. He runs the big fruit stall at the markets. She helps him sometimes. They have four *kinner* now."

"Four?" Beverly didn't even have a boyfriend anymore, and with the two friends she'd grown up with being mothers, she felt she was missing out. Being twenty-eight, she was well aware of her biological clock ticking. She wanted her children to have a young mother, not parents who were old enough to be their grandparents. "Do you think she'd mind if I visited her?"

"I think she'd like that. She only lives ten minutes from here. They bought the old Strongberger *haus* down by the mill."

"I'll try to get there today some time. I can't wait to see her again. And that's great news about your son and Betsy getting married."

"*Jah,* I thought he was going to remain about the *haus* forever and then they got married just like that." She clicked her fingers in the air.

"How often do you work here?"

"In the busy season, I work every day. Now I only come here to clean once a week. And, now that you're all grown up you must call me Dora."

Beverly giggled. "Okay, Dora it is." Beverly figured Dora probably needed the income. The downturn of the bed-and-breakfast was far-reaching and affected more people than just Jeremiah and Janet. "Who does the outside maintenance? The gardening for example?"

"They didn't have just one regular person. They had different people do the gardens and the lawn. Then Jeremiah was trying to do everything himself when times got tight."

"Resulting in him falling off the roof."

"That's right."

Janet walked into the room and shot them a disapproving look.

"I better get on with it, Beverly. I'm glad you're back," Dora said.

"It's only for a few weeks," she was quick to assure her.

Dora picked up the mop and continued her task.

A flood of guilt washed over Beverly. She could've contacted her two good friends— written to them at least.

After Janet had made David and Beverly a large breakfast of pancakes with maple syrup, David and Beverly walked out to hitch the buggy for their morning excursion.

"The horse is called Trevor."

David laughed. "Is he?"

"Yes. Janet assures me she's not responsible for the name. He was called Trevor by the previous owners."

"I'd reckon there's a story behind that one."

Beverly grinned, and then watched as David hitched the buggy. Concentration filled his face and Beverly studied every contour—the straight line of his nose, his strong jawline, and his high cheekbones.

Once he was finished, he smiled and looked over at her. "Ready to go?"

"Yes."

They both climbed in and headed off down the road.

"I know you came here to get away, but why here?"

"I felt like a break, so when Bishop Eli's letter arrived, I jumped at the chance to see this part of the country. I've never been here before."

"It is beautiful out here. It's something I never appreciated while I was growing up here. So, are you a relative of Bishop Eli? I know Janet is."

"Janet's mother and the bishop's *mudder* were sisters. My *mudder* is Janet's *schweschder*."

"Ah, so you and Eli are second cousins?"

He shook his head. "I don't think so. Maybe. It muddles my head to try to figure it all out sometimes. I'm thinking someone told me we're first cousins, once removed."

"My head swirls with that stuff, too." That meant he and Janet were fairly closely related. Beverly had hoped they were distant relatives. "Does your mother have a similar personality to Janet?"

"Nee, they're nothing alike. Janet was the eldest and *Mamm* was the youngest."

Beverly nodded again. "Twelve in the family, you said?"

"That's right."

"There would be quite an age distance between them."

"Jah, there is."

"That explains Janet's bossiness." Beverly gasped. "Oh, that just slipped out."

He laughed. "That's okay. I'm not going to repeat it."

"Good. Please don't."

. . .

THEY ARRIVED at the first guesthouse, just five miles away from Jeremiah's.

"Here it is." David pulled the buggy off to the side of the road and stopped where they had a good view.

"I remember this house. I visited someone here when I was a child. I think I went with *Mamm.* It would've been refurbished since then. I don't see this place being much competition. It's too small."

After they both looked at it from the buggy for a moment, David asked, "Seen enough?"

"Yes, on to the next."

The next one was two miles from that one and closer to the town center. The roads had become much busier just in that short distance, as two roads merged into the one they were on.

"I'll have to keep going. There's nowhere

to stop here. I can stop up further and we can walk back."

"Okay."

When they stopped, David said, "I'll stay with the buggy; there's nowhere to hitch Trevor. You go back."

Beverly grinned again at the horse's unusual name. "Okay. I won't be long."

She walked back past the bed-and-breakfast. It looked nice, bright and cheerful, and it was close to everything and probably had all the modern conveniences. Also, it was well-cared for and looked immaculate. After she had satisfied herself that she'd had a good look, she headed back to David.

"Well, I must say it's bigger than the last one," Beverly said when she climbed up next to David.

"Almost as big as ours," he said.

"And the gardens are so lovely. That's where our place falls down. First impression. It doesn't even look nice now because the gardens have been let go. It used to look so attractive. My mother was always out in the garden in the spring and the summer."

"*Jah,* that place looked much more impressive. Where to now?"

"Back home."

"Okay." He waited until there were no cars and turned the buggy around.

"What are you helping the bishop to do today?"

"I'm helping out doing a bit of carpentry work. For some reason, Eli thinks I'm a carpenter."

Beverly laughed. "Just like Janet. I wonder why they both think that?"

He smiled. "I can turn my hand to most things."

"We'll have to take full advantage of you while you're here. You must tell the bishop that he can't take up all your time."

He looked over at her.

"Well isn't that why you're here?" she

asked. "To help Janet, not the bishop?"

"*Jah,* and the bishop knows that. I don't think he'll be asking me again. This was just something spontaneous."

"Good."

When they got back home the place was empty except for Dora, who told them that Jeremiah and Janet had gone to a check-up at the hospital. When the bishop arrived to take David away, Beverly went to ask more questions of Dora.

"Dora, they said nothing to me about going to the hospital. Is he okay?"

"It's just a regular check-up. That's what they told me."

"They went in a taxi?"

Dora nodded.

"I wish they would've told me and I would've gone too." Just as the words came out of her mouth she knew that's why Janet hadn't told her. Janet wanted to go alone with Jeremiah.

"I'll be here until late this afternoon, so why don't you take my buggy and visit Leah? She doesn't live far."

"Would you mind?"

"Of course not. Go ahead."

"Thanks Dora." She turned back around and headed out to Dora's buggy. It brought back memories of being in the driver's seat as a young girl, holding the leather reins in her hands. A strange urge came over her to drive the buggy fast. She resisted the urge and set a slow steady pace. She hadn't forgotten how to drive a buggy.

An image came into her mind of Leah as she was ten years ago. She regretted not calling to say goodbye, but the argument with Janet hadn't been planned and neither had her sudden departure from the community.

Now she'd find out how Leah's life had turned out and how she handled four young children.

CHAPTER 10

WHEN THE BUGGY pulled up into Leah's driveway, Beverly knew Leah had visitors. Several, judging by the two buggies outside her house. Once she had secured Dora's buggy, she headed toward the house, hoping Leah would still talk to her. Maybe she wouldn't be pleased to see her because she'd left the community, and wouldn't feel right talking to her. Even though Beverly hadn't been shunned, she was officially an outsider.

A woman she didn't recognize, looked

out the window and then she heard someone say, "It's Jeremiah's daughter."

The door swung open and Leah rushed out. Her old friend had barely changed. If anything, she was more beautiful and she was clearly pleased to see her.

They hugged warmly, and then Beverly stepped back and looked at her. "You haven't changed a bit."

"Neither have you. Except you're much thinner."

"I've lost the puppy fat," Beverly said and they both giggled.

"Are you back to stay or to visit?"

"I'm back to help my father with the bed-and-breakfast and then I'll be leaving."

"Come inside. I've got visitors, but they were just leaving."

"Anyone I know?"

"Molly and Mildred King."

Beverly nodded. She remembered the two elderly sisters-in-law.

As they walked to the house, Leah said, "We have a sewing circle and everyone's left but those two; they are always the last to leave."

Molly and Mildred left very quickly after they said hello to Beverly.

Beverly looked out the window at them as they made their way to their separate buggies. "Was it something I said?"

Leah giggled. "You're not in the community anymore. I'd say they don't want to talk to you."

"I guess I can understand that. Now where are these four children I've been hearing about?"

"Three are at school and the *boppli's* asleep."

"You have a baby, how sweet! I feel so old. You have children old enough for school?"

"Jah, I do."

"Can I see the baby?"

"Sure. His name's Adam. He's six months old. Whatever you do don't wake him."

Beverly nodded and then followed Leah to the end of the hall. The baby's bedroom was the last one.

Leah pushed the door open and Beverly crept in. He was much bigger than Beverly had expected. He lay on his side with one chubby cheek squashed into a small pillow, causing his mouth to open.

"He's so cute," Beverly whispered. They backed away and Leah closed the door quietly.

"Can I make you coffee or something?"

"Yes please. Coffee would be good."

As they sat on the couch in the living room, Leah said, "You never wrote."

She shook her head. "I'm so sorry. I wrote to *Dat* and he didn't write back. Then I thought it would be a bit weird to be writing to someone else when *Dat* wasn't answering me. Then I eventually stopped writing to him. I had to leave my old life behind me if I was to survive."

"What happened? Betsy and I asked your *vadder*, but he would never answer a question directly. All he said was that you left suddenly."

"I had a big argument with Janet."

"But you had those all the time."

"This one was a really big one—the biggest. I said some cruel things to her—horrible things." She sipped her coffee from the thin china teacup. "I can't even tell you what caused the outburst now."

"It must have been awful. Where did you go?"

"New York City, and that's where I live now. I work in a bank there. It's a good life. Now tell me, how did it come about that Betsy married Levi Stoltzfus?"

Leah breathed out heavily. "She was in love with an *Englischer* and she was sneaking out to see him and that ended dreadfully; she was heartbroken. Levi helped her through it and eventually, well actually pretty quickly, she fell in love with him."

"How did the two of them end up talking? He was so much older than us."

"She had a slight accident in her buggy and was on the side of the road until Levi came along. It was just after she had ended things with Cameron, and she told Levi everything."

Beverly shook her head. "I can't imagine the two of them together."

"She's in love with him. And he's in love with her. It was a real love match. And she said it was strange because he's the total opposite of Cameron."

"Why did they move to Ohio?"

"How do you know all these things?"

"Dora works at the bed-and-breakfast."

"That's right, of course."

"She told me where you live and everything. Even let me use her buggy to drive here."

"They moved so he could work for his *onkel*. They come back every few months. You might even see her while you're here. She's due for a visit about now."

"Oh, I'd like that."

"And how are things with you and Janet now?" Leah asked.

Slowly, Beverly shook her head. "Nothing much has changed. I'm glad I'm back here, though. It's good to see *Dat*. Janet has a nephew there to help as well. I think she wanted someone on her team. No, that can't be right because he was asked to come before she knew I was coming."

"Is it David Hilty?"

"That's him. How do you know him?"

"I know his girlfriend."

"He's got a girlfriend?"

"*Jah*. Her name's Susan."

"Oh,"

"You didn't know?"

"No, I didn't. It's a wonder Janet didn't make sure I knew."

"Like that, is it? Does she think you're fond of him?"

Beverly shrugged her shoulders. "I don't know."

Leah leaned forward. "Do you like him?"

"No, there's no point in me liking anyone who's Amish. I'll never return to the community." She didn't mention she also had met and liked Oscar, and she was seeing him that very afternoon.

"That's a shame."

"That's how things are. I've got a whole new life now."

"Tell me about it."

Beverly spent the next half hour telling Leah everything about her life and then the baby cried. "Sounds like someone's awake."

Beverly walked in with Leah while she

picked Adam up out of the crib, and then she looked on as Leah changed his diaper.

"Have you ever changed a diaper before?"

"Never, and todays' not going to be the first day I do."

Leah laughed. "Come with me to the kitchen while I warm up his bottle."

"How do you do that without a microwave?"

Leah giggled. "I set it in hot water from the kettle."

"Oh."

"Don't judge me. I tried breastfeeding and it wasn't for me."

"I'm the last one to judge about anything."

"You've sure been gone a long time."

"Ten years is a long time."

"Would you like to hold him?"

"I'd love to. As long as he doesn't cry."

"He normally doesn't. He might if he's really hungry, and that's all."

"If he does I'm giving him straight back." Beverly put her arms out for the baby and Leah passed him over. As soon as he was in her arms, her maternal instinct kicked in. She held him close and cuddled him against her, and the baby rested his head on her shoulder.

"Oh, you two look so cute together."

"I want one of these," Beverly said.

"You should find yourself a husband."

"I've been looking."

"I'm surprised you're not married by now."

"I've only had ever had one real boyfriend. That didn't end well. He went back to his previous girlfriend and then they married."

"How awful. You must've been devastated."

"It wasn't a pleasant experience. Especially given that we were engaged and making plans. It was nice to have someone special in my life. Now I don't miss him so much, but I do miss sharing things with someone and being a part of a couple."

Leah popped the bottle of milk into a saucepan of warm water. "I'm sure you'll find someone."

"I thought I would've found someone before now. I don't know, maybe it wasn't meant to be."

"I'm sure you'll find someone," Leah repeated.

"I should get back. Janet's taken *Dat* to the hospital for a check up and I want to get there when they return, before they return."

"Janet will be missing you?"

Beverly laughed. "Not missing me in that way, that's for sure and for certain."

"You'll come back and visit me before you go, won't you?"

"Yes, I'll have to meet your other children if I can."

"I'd love that. I'll tell you what, why don't you and David come to dinner?"

"Really?"

"*Jah,* Friday night?"

"Okay, thank you. What time?"

"We have dinner early. Make it for six?"

"Okay. What if David can't come?"

"Can you come alone?"

"All right. I'll be looking forward to it." Reluctantly, Beverly handed back the baby. "I'll see you on Friday night then."

"I'm so glad you're back."

"It's so good to see you." Beverly gave her a smile before she headed out of the house.

CHAPTER 11

WHEN BEVERLY GOT BACK HOME she walked into the kitchen for a glass of water. She came to a stop, surprised to see David sitting at the table eating a sandwich.

"What are you doing back so soon?"

He finished eating what was in his mouth. "It was only a small job and there were about six others there, so we were able to do everything fairly quickly."

"I thought you'd be gone for ages."

"Me too."

She walked to the sink and helped herself

to that glass of water. As she sipped on it, she turned around and leaned against the sink facing David. "I was just visiting a friend of mine, Leah. She's invited you and me to have dinner at her place on Friday night."

"Leah Yoder?"

"I guess that's her last name now. She said she knows you, but she didn't say where she met you."

"I met Leah and Benjamin at a wedding recently. I've been looking forward to seeing them again."

"Good. I'll tell them we're coming on Friday night, okay?"

"*Jah.*"

When they heard a car, Beverly said, "That must be them back from the hospital." Beverly placed her glass on the counter and hurried to find out what the outcome of the doctor's visit was. She opened the door and watched as Janet helped Jeremiah out of the taxi. Then she moved forward to help.

JEREMIAH'S DAUGHTER (AMISH ROMANCE)

"It's all right. I've got him," Janet said snappishly.

"How did the appointment go?"

"I'm doing well," Jeremiah said.

That didn't tell Beverly much. "That's good." Beverly moved back out of the way and waited on the porch. Using his crutches, her father slowly made his way to the house while Janet stayed close by his side.

As they past Beverly, Janet said, "We had a long wait and your *vadder's* worn out. He's going to have a sleep."

"Okay. I've got that meeting with Oscar soon." She noticed a car moving toward the house. "Oh, here he is already."

"Be home by dinner," Janet said.

"I will."

Beverly went inside to get her handbag and when she was nearly back at the front door, David came up behind her. "Is he going to name a price for the place?"

"I'll find out how much he's willing to pay. That might sway *Dat* and Janet to sell."

"You want them to sell?"

"Not exactly. I want them to have an easier life, and I don't think it's easy for them slaving away here. Especially since the business is not doing well."

She smiled at him and then headed out to meet Oscar. She was glad they weren't going out for dinner because she hadn't brought any suitable clothes. She'd only brought casual daywear.

He jumped out of the car and opened the passenger door for her.

"Thank you."

He closed the door and went around to his side and slid in next to her. "I didn't think your aunt would let you come," he said as his car hummed down the driveway.

She buckled her seatbelt. "She's my stepmother, not my aunt."

"Ah."

"Where are we going?"

"A local bar." He glanced at her. "Don't worry, they serve coffee too. I won't get you intoxicated."

"That's comforting to know. Are you staying with your parents while you're here?"

"They moved on some time ago. They're in Atlanta now."

"Where are you staying?"

"At a bed-and-breakfast."

"Which one?" She wondered why he hadn't stayed at the Beilers,' since he wanted to buy it. It would have been a logical thing to do.

"It's not far from here, Iris Guest House."

"How are you finding it?"

"Adequate."

It was the first place she and David had driven past earlier in the day.

"Why don't you buy it?"

He threw his head back and laughed. "It's got no character."

"Why didn't you stay at my parents' bed-and-breakfast if you're interested in buying it?"

"I didn't know it was still operating as a guest house."

"What makes you say that?"

"I couldn't find it on the Internet."

Beverly groaned.

He glanced at her. "What's the matter?"

She breathed out heavily. "I've been trying to tell them that."

"Their lifestyle would make things difficult to run a business, wouldn't it?"

"Yes. They're not Old Order Amish, but they're conservative."

"Most of the Amish around here are."

"You know a bit about the Amish?" she asked, brows raised in surprise.

"Yeah, hard to avoid, growing up next

door to them. What made you leave?" he asked.

"A number of things." She didn't want to go into it and tell him she'd had a big fight with her stepmother.

"How often do you visit?"

"This is the first time in ten years." She couldn't tell him the bed-and-breakfast was failing. In fact, she'd probably already said too much. If he thought it wasn't doing so well he'd surely offer a lower price. "My father isn't well. He broke his leg and I came back to help Janet run the place. They're both getting older, so I thought selling the place is one option. That's why I agreed to hear what you've got to say."

He took his eyes off the road and glanced over at her again. "What? You mean, this isn't a date?"

She could tell by his crooked smile he knew it wasn't. "No." She giggled.

"You could've let me down gently."

"I'm a straightforward person. I always say what I mean."

"Good. I'll know where I stand."

"What kind of law do you do?" She'd meant to Google him from her smart phone, but she hadn't gotten around to it. Besides, the battery was most likely dead by now.

"Anything but family law—divorces, and custody issues. It's too messy and I hate it when children are involved."

That showed Beverly that he was a caring person and had a love of children. That earned him another tick.

ONCE THEY WERE SITTING at a small table in the back of the bar, Oscar locked eyes with her. "I'm surprised we haven't met before. Do you go out much?"

"Not much these days."

He took a sip of coffee. "How did you go from being an Amish girl to working as a loans manager? I know the Amish aren't big on education."

"I left when I was eighteen."

"That would've been hard. You would've been little more than a child yourself."

"That's true. I ended up sharing an apartment in Harlem. That's where I ended up; it wasn't the best, but back then I had to make do. I did various courses while I worked in a fast food restaurant. After two years, I got a job in the bank as an assistant and worked my way up from there. It's not that exciting, but it pays the bills and I work with a good crowd of people." She took a sip of coffee hoping it wouldn't keep her awake all night. "That sums me up. What about you?"

His blue eyes twinkled. "I'm too boring to talk about."

"I doubt that. Tell me what you did after college."

"I went straight into the firm I'm working at now. I'd been a student intern there, and

they were happy enough with my perfor-
mance to offer me a job. There's not much
more to tell."

Beverly wondered if he was hiding something. Was he married? He wanted to hear
about her, and revealed nothing about himself. "Did you have an offer in mind for my
father's house?"

"How much land does he have?"

"Forty acres."

He raised his eyebrows. "The land runs
down to the river?"

"Yes. The boundary is just the other side
of the river, and the road running along the
front is the other boundary line. Well, just before it. It's a rectangular shaped plot of land.
A lane runs along the length of the border."

"I've seen the plat."

He was full of surprises. "Where?"

"I made inquiries."

That showed Beverly he was serious

about buying it. "If you've already made inquiries, you would know where the boundaries are."

He chuckled. "That's true. I'm talking too much because you make me nervous."

"I do?"

He nodded. "I had no intention of letting you know that I saw the plat." He took another sip of coffee. "I talk in court all the time before vicious judges and other lawyers out to cut me down, but there's something about you that makes me nervous." He wagged his finger at her.

That made her giggle. "I don't know why."

"You should. You're captivating, and I've never seen such beautiful pale blue eyes."

She looked away from him and then cleared her throat. In an effort to bring the conversation back to business, she asked, "Do you have a number?"

"I gave you my business card; my number's on that."

Beverly laughed. "No, I didn't mean your phone number, I meant a price that you would offer my father."

"Ah." He chuckled. "I've got a one-track mind when I'm in front of a beautiful woman."

Beverly could feel heat rising to her cheeks. She didn't want to blush like a schoolgirl, but she feared she was.

"The number is whatever it would take for them to sell."

"Do you mean you want *them* to name a figure?"

"Yes. I'll pay a fair price, but I need you to convince them to sell."

She drew her eyebrows together. "Why would I do that?"

"You said yourself they'd be better off selling the place, considering their ages."

"I said they might be better off. They'll

need a good price. They only have the house and property, and that's all. They don't have any other savings. In order to sell, they'd have to be able to buy a smaller place and live off the rest of the sale amount. It could be a good money earner if you put someone in to manage it and put it with the major booking websites."

"I know. I'm aware of the potential. I just want it as an escape—a getaway. Somewhere quiet I can come to gather my thoughts. Now that doesn't mean I can't pay them a handsome sum. Anyway, why don't you see what they say? They can name their price, and then we can go from there."

He wasn't making things easy for her. It would've been better if he had named a price that would blow them away and encourage them to sell. Now she had no offer with which to go back to them. Unless, she could draw one out of him. "Do you know of any recent sales in the area?"

"I've been keeping an eye on the prices. It's been a long-term goal of mine to buy back into the area."

"Why don't you name a figure, and then I'll have something to go back to them with?"

He shook his head and his face grew rigid, like stone. "I don't want to go back and forth. I want them to name the price that they want and if I can manage it, I'll do it."

In one way, she admired that. He was a man not wanting to be mucked around trying to drive down the price. "I can appreciate that, but I've also got to talk them into selling. Don't you think you could give me some bait?"

"Ah, like going fishing?"

"Yes. Something to entice them."

"No. I have every confidence in you that you'll make them see sense. From the looks of the place they haven't being doing too well. How long can they continue like that?"

He knew! "I'll see what I can do." She liked his no nonsense approach.

"Good. Now tell me more about yourself. Why's a girl like you still single?"

"Who said I was?"

"You're not wearing a ring, and you agreed to come out with me."

"I could ask you the same thing." She hoped he wasn't about to say he was married.

"I've been too wound up in my work. In time, I'll take things easier. I've just made partner and I thought things would ease up, but I've been busier than ever."

"Congratulations. Your parents must be proud."

"They are."

"Do you have siblings?"

"Two older brothers. One's in the army and one's an artist studying in France."

"You're all so different."

"Yes." He drained the last of his coffee,

which reminded her she'd hardly touched hers.

If her father refused to get a loan, they'd have no choice but to sell. As far as Beverly could see, the man in front of her was a God-send—for her father and Janet as well as for herself.

"Would your aunt, err... stepmother mind if you had dinner with me tonight? I know a lovely place—"

"Tonight's out of the question. I'm sorry. We have visitors coming for dinner."

"Tomorrow night? Is that too soon?"

"I've got your number, why don't I call you after I have a talk with my father and Janet?"

"Okay." He glanced at his wristwatch. "How much longer do you have?"

"I should be getting back about now. In time for dinner. Thanks for the coffee."

He chuckled. "I wish it was dinner."

She would've preferred dinner too, so she could've found out more about him.

He drove back slowly and she imagined his reason for going so slow was because he wanted to be with her longer. "What do you do while you're here?" she asked.

"I'm ashamed to say that I'm still doing a little work while I'm here. Sorting out a few things for clients."

"Not much of a break then, is it?"

"I guess not, but I find it hard to stop. I'm not the kind of person who can do nothing. That's why your parents' house appeals to me. I think I'd be able to shut out the world and be still for a moment."

"It's certainly quiet there."

"See if you can change their minds, would you?"

"I'll do my best."

"Thank you." He stopped the car by the house.

"I'll talk to my father now. Janet will be busy in the kitchen, I'd say."

"Is he the decision maker?"

"I'm not sure. It's probably fifty-fifty. I'm thinking that if either one changes their mind, they'll be able to talk the other one into it. I'll be in touch."

"Beverly, maybe you should set up a meeting for me with them."

"No. That wouldn't work. Definitely not. I'll talk to them. Leave it with me."

"You'll let me know?"

"Yes. I'll call you in a day or two."

"Thanks, Beverly."

She opened the door, and once she was out, she turned around and closed it. The passenger window lowered. She leaned down so she could see him. "I'll see you later, Oscar. Thanks again."

"I'll see you soon. And you're welcome."

She walked to the house, listening to the gentle hum as his car moved away.

CHAPTER 12

As soon as she walked into the house, she heard Janet and David talking in the kitchen. She took the opportunity to slip upstairs to speak with her father.

The door was open and he was just getting back into bed. "Been doing your exercises?"

"*Jah,* I was doing a little. I got into trouble with the doctor today for not doing them."

She stepped forward and helped him get back under the blankets.

"Janet tells me you were at a meeting with someone who wants to buy this place?"

"That's right I was. I've just come back from talking with him. He said he's willing to pay you a very good price."

"Well, did he say how much is a very good price?"

"He wants you to come up with a figure."

"This place is priceless."

"True, in your heart, but just because you're emotionally attached to the place doesn't make it priceless."

"It is to me."

"I explained that you need to make enough to buy another place and live off the rest. Just to give him an idea of the amount of money he has to offer."

"But he's not offering, is he? He wants you to offer first."

"That's right. Look, *Dat,* I've got some savings—"

"I'd never take money from you. It's the

parents who look after the *kinner,* not the other way around."

"It's the other way around when parents get older. The children look after the parents. Isn't that why you and *Mamm* had me?"

Jeremiah chuckled, and right at that moment Janet walked into the room.

She set her eyes upon Beverly. "Is that your sense of humor again, Beverly?"

"Yes, it is."

"Beverly was offering us money and I told her we'd never touch her money."

"Nee, we wouldn't."

Beverly knew they both had their own reasons for not wanting to borrow the money from her.

"Well, as far as I can see, there only three choices—actually, only two. You either have to make this place work again or you have to sell it. And to make this place work...well, you can't do it without a loan. If you don't want to borrow from the bank, how about looking for another investor?"

"Does that mean someone else will own this place besides us?" Janet asked.

"Yes. Or in partnership with you."

"I wouldn't like that. This is our home."

"They are the choices you have."

"Beverly's right," her father said.

"Give us a couple of days to think about this."

"While you're thinking about it, why don't I approach your bank and see if they will lend you the money? Because if they won't lend you the money, then you're only left with the other option."

"*Gott* will make a way," Janet said.

"Yeah, and his way is one of these three: to sell off, get a loan, or get an investor."

Jeremiah said, "Say if we get a loan and fix this place up, then what?"

"We'll have a relaunch party and invite people in the tourist industry and from local businesses who might have people who stay in the area from time to time. We could also invite the booking websites and see if they can help in any way."

"What do you think, Janet?" Jeremiah asked.

"I don't want to move away."

Jeremiah looked back at Beverly. "Okay, go see someone at the bank."

"All right. I'll need you to sign some kind of authority for me to ask questions on your behalf. What bank are you with?" When he told her she froze. It was the same bank that her ex worked for. Of course, he wouldn't be at that branch, but she didn't need to be reminded of him.

Jeremiah went on to say, "Just organize it and I'll sign whatever you want. We'll think about a loan when you find out the finer details."

At last, Beverly felt like she was getting somewhere.

"Denke for helping us, Beverly."

That was the first time Janet had thanked her for anything. Ever. She was sure of that. "I'll do what I can," Beverly uttered with a nod before she hurried out of her father's room.

CHAPTER 13

It was another awkward dinner with Janet. All Beverly wanted to do was talk to David in private and find out more about him. If she talked in front of Janet, she'd be accused again of throwing herself at him. She ate her lamb and potato stew in silence.

"How did your meeting with the lawyer go?" David asked her.

"I think it went well, but I couldn't get a price out of him."

David said, "The number one law in negotiation is make the other person name a price first."

"Is that so?" Janet asked.

He smiled and nodded. "So I've heard, but he's a lawyer and not a salesman. He might not know those rules."

"Aren't all lawyers like snake oil salesmen?" Janet asked.

"So cynical, Janet." Beverly giggled.

"I'm just going on what I've heard about them."

"I think we need to give Mr Reynolds the benefit of the doubt," Beverly said.

Janet's eyes bulged wide. "I'd rather be cautious."

"Anyway, as soon as the bank opens tomorrow, I'm going to set up an appointment. Hopefully, I can see them tomorrow to get things started."

Janet raised a finger in the air. "We haven't agreed to it yet."

"I understand. I'm just finding out things

at this stage."

"Very good."

"Would you like me to drive you in?" David asked.

"Yes please, if it wouldn't be too much trouble."

David turned to Janet. "Can we borrow your buggy and Trevor again, Aunt Janet?"

"Of course. They're both at your disposal while you're here."

"*Denke.*"

BEVERLY SUCCEEDED in getting an appointment at the bank in the early afternoon. David drove her in, and several minutes before Beverly was supposed to be there he found a parking spot close to the bank.

"Shall I wait here?" he asked.

"If you want. It might take half an hour to an hour."

"If I'm not here when you come back I

won't be far away. I'll just be stretching my legs."

"Okay. Send me good thoughts."

"I'll pray for you."

She laughed and felt bad for not suggesting it herself. "Even better." She got out of the buggy with the paperwork in hand and breathed in deeply. It would be awful if she walked into the bank and saw the man who'd dumped her. Kevin was based in the city branch, so he shouldn't be here, but that didn't stop her from worrying.

Once inside the bank, she was quickly ushered into a glass-walled office with a desk, two chairs, and one computer. A few minutes later, a short, balding spectacle-wearing man walked in and introduced himself as Noel Worthington.

After he went over the figures, Mr. Worthington estimated what the property was worth. He had no problem loaning them ten thousand dollars, and said he would even approve loaning them more if they needed it. Beverly thanked him and said she'd need to talk things over with her father.

When she got back to the buggy, David wasn't there. Looking around, she still couldn't see him anywhere so she walked up the street. After looking in a few store windows, she finally found him in a paint store.

"Just browsing, are you?" she asked as she poked him in the ribs.

He jumped and turned to her. "I didn't think you'd be out so soon."

"I've been looking everywhere for you."

"I'm sorry. I just get lost in hardware stores."

"I'm like that with shoes. Maybe we should take a few of those paint charts with us."

"*Jah,* okay. Are they going to loan the money?"

"They had no problem with it. I thought it would be fine. It's not a huge amount, and if they need more the banker said they could have it."

He grimaced. "The more they borrow, the more they'll have to pay back."

"True, and they don't like even borrowing a small amount."

He leaned over and took some color charts. "Just in case Jeremiah agrees to the loan. It'll save time getting started."

"Good." Beverly couldn't see any other way. Even if they decided to sell, they'd still have to spruce the house up, and painting was the cheapest way of doing that.

WHEN THEY GOT BACK HOME, Beverly ran up the stairs, excited to tell her father that the bank had approved the loan in principle. "It's good news, *Dat.*"

"We can get a loan, Petal?"

"Yes." She moved closer and sat on the edge of his bed.

"I don't know if we'll need it."

"What do you mean?"

"That man came here again and had a good talk with Janet."

"What man?"

"The lawyer from New York."

Anger rippled through Beverly. She thought Oscar and she had an understanding. He hadn't listened to her instructions. How dare he! She hid her anger from her father. "He came here?"

"He left about half an hour ago."

It occurred to Beverly that he might've been sneaking around, watching the place, and seen her leave. "Did he make an offer?"

"Janet forced an offer out of him. It seems a lot of money and Janet is considering it."

Beverly didn't know what to say.

"What's wrong now?" he asked. "You were all for selling yesterday."

"I just want to make sure it's the right move for you. We have to consider everything. Would you be bored if you didn't have the bed-and-breakfast?"

"I'm bored now and it hasn't killed me. I've been awfully bored these last days." He rubbed his beard.

"A smaller house wouldn't need much maintenance."

"I can't make a decision right now. Janet and I need to think about it and pray on it."

"Okay." She didn't think it was a good idea to delay things. They needed to act fast since they were already losing money, but if she pushed them, she'd be blamed if they regretted their decision.

He continued, "Janet wouldn't let him look through the house and he still gave a good offer. Janet thinks he'll pay more money after you paint the rooms and fix them up."

"Oh, so she still wants to go ahead with all that?"

"I think so. How much will it cost?"

"It depends upon exactly what you want to do."

"Janet told me what's on your list, with the new quilts and some new pieces of furniture, and that you wanted to paint all the rooms."

"Ten thousand dollars should cover it, and if we don't spend that much we can always pay it back to the bank against the loan."

"Thanks for finding out about all that and for going to the bank."

"That's why I'm here, *Dat.*"

"Ten thousand seems a lot of money for paints, but I'll take your word for it."

"It's not just paint. It's new furniture, and quilts, and tidying up the garden."

"You're the one with a head for finance. Did you see Janet downstairs?"

"I think she's in the kitchen. I came straight up here. I'll tell her what I learned, shall I?"

Her father nodded.

Beverly headed down the stairs to find out exactly what Oscar had said.

It unnerved her that Oscar had come when she wasn't there. She had made it plain to him that he was to talk to her and not Janet or Jeremiah. He wasn't what he seemed, and now she knew that he was trouble.

Janet was in the kitchen kneading dough.

"Janet, *Dat* says that Oscar Reynolds was here."

Her face lit up. "He was here. He had a list of similar properties and what they had sold for. The price he offered was higher than those."

"*Dat* said you didn't accept?"

"*Nee.* We haven't decided what to do yet. And I told your *vadder* that we'll have him back here when the place is all painted up nicely and then we'll see if he offers more."

"You and *Dat* said you'd leave the negotiations up to me."

"We haven't started negotiating yet. I agree. You do it, I don't want to."

Beverly relaxed. She didn't want Janet or her father to be taken advantage of by a hotshot lawyer from the city. "I don't think you should let him in again if I'm not here. I told him I would talk to you both, and then I'd call him in a day or two." Beverly put her hands on her hips. "He's completely disregarded what I said."

"Don't be too hard on him. I think he just likes the place so much that he couldn't wait."

"Don't you be too nice, or he might be around here all the time harassing the both of you."

"Do you think so?"

Beverly nodded. "Anyway, the bank has no problem loaning you the money, and more if you want."

"That is good news."

"It sounds like you want to go ahead with the renovations either way?"

"*Jah*, and I know someone who makes lovely quilts. She's got a few for sale right now."

"Good. Find out how much they are, would you?"

"I can find out tomorrow."

"Wonderful. I've got paperwork that you and *Dat* will have to sign and I'll take it back to the bank tomorrow and then I'll get the paint and look at a couple of furniture stores."

"Can we get the money right away?"

"If we can't, I'll use my money and you can pay me back. Okay?"

"I don't know about that."

"Relax. I'll keep track of what everything costs and you can pay me back when the loan money comes through."

"Do you have that kind of money?"

"I've been saving for a deposit on a small apartment."

"Good for you. Does that mean you've given up the idea of marriage?"

"If it happens it happens. I'm not going hunting for a husband." She headed out the room, not comfortable talking to Janet about such things.

CHAPTER 14

ON FRIDAY MORNING, David took Beverly to the stores.

"You can help choose," Beverly said when they walked into the first furniture store.

"I can't do that."

"You must," Beverly urged.

"*Nee.*"

"That won't do at all. Janet brought you here to help. You must help with the ... all the choices."

"Oh, I see where you're coming from. You

want a scapegoat just in case Janet doesn't like what we choose."

"No, no, that's not it at all."

He chuckled. "I think it is, but I'm warning you, I have no taste. If I like something, you must choose the opposite."

"What about your *bruder's* bed-and-breakfast? Are the rooms there nicely furnished and decorated?"

"*Jah,* but his *fraa* did that. It had nothing to do with me. We must have this decision-making business sorted out. I can give you an opinion on what *you* select. How's that?"

She nodded. "Okay, I can live with that."

"And that saves us both from getting into trouble," he added with a smirk.

"I don't know why Janet didn't want to do this herself."

"She already did. That's why we have to fix what she's done. You can see the results there now. She took all the Amish quilts out, and all the other things just aren't homey-feeling yet."

"Yes, that's true. We're fixing her selections." She sighed. It was a lot of responsibility.

"I'm behind you. I'm not in front of you, mind you, but I'll be behind you."

She laughed at that line. His comments showed Beverly that he, too, was scared of Janet. She felt better not being the only one. As they walked around looking at the furniture, Beverly said, "Tell me something, is your *bruder's* bed-and-breakfast listed with all the booking websites?"

"Of course."

"We'll have to arrange that somehow."

He stopped still and folded his arms across his chest. "Their bishop won't allow it. I know some allow them for businesses, but Eli won't."

"That puts them at a disadvantage. Do you know about computers?"

"*Jah.* I had to learn because I had to help my *bruder.*"

"I think it's funny how the Amish want to remain separate and yet many of the Amish businesses have websites and electrical power to the businesses, but just not their homes. Does that strike you as funny?"

"Not at all. Every bishop has his own way of doing things. Every business needs to survive. Our lives have no influences of the outside world and we remain separate. It's just in our work lives that some of the bishops allows these things, for commercial purposes only."

"I know, I just think it's a little weird or hypocritical, that's all. Either you want to be separate or you don't."

"It's a matter of making money to live, that's all."

"I realize that. In regard to making money, we are willing to mix with the outside world to take their money from them."

"I think you're trying to pick fault with the Amish in general. You want them to have a computer and Wi-Fi but if they do, you'll be critical of them for not being separate and sticking to their values."

"Maybe you're right."

He chuckled. "You give up your argument pretty quickly."

Beverly smiled and shook her head. "I'm too tired to argue."

"And no matter what you and I think, it will have little bearing on what the bishops do in the various communities."

"That's true. Maybe one day you'll be made a bishop."

He laughed. "I highly doubt that."

"Yes, but you never know. The bishop from your community might die and when they're choosing another one the lot might fall on you. Then what will you do?"

"Become a bishop, I guess."

"How would you feel about it?"

"I don't know. I'll save the thinking about it for when it happens, if it happens, but I've got a feeling it won't. And I'll have to be married first."

She was getting along too well with him. Out of the blue, when they were just about to decide between two chests of drawers, she blurted out, "Is your girlfriend okay with you being away from her while you're here?"

He startled, and stared at her for a moment. "We're no longer together."

"Oh, I'm sorry! I didn't know. Leah mentioned she knew your girlfriend and ... I'm ... I'm so sorry. I shouldn't have said anything."

"It's okay. I can talk about it. She decided she liked someone else better. That's all there is to it."

"Really?"

He chuckled. "I'd like to think you're surprised because you can't imagine anyone better than me."

"It's not that, I'm sorry. It's just that it's exactly the same thing that happened to me."

He raised his eyebrows. "Then you know how it feels to be walked out on." He sighed. "I thought we were suited; she was the one who thought we weren't."

That's exactly how it'd been between herself and Kevin. "I can relate."

"We weren't far off marrying."

"Me too. Well, there was a ring. I suppose you could say I was engaged. I've still got the ring. I tried to give it back. I should mail it to him."

"*Jah,* you should."

"I will. It's not a nice reminder to have. We hadn't got as far as telling his parents, or mine, and he suddenly went back to his ex-girlfriend." She brushed her hair away from her face. "They're married now."

"I'm sorry to hear that."

"Me too. Not now, but I was back then. It

took me a while to get over It. It's just that it's not easy for me to get close to someone."

"Why's that?"

Beverly shrugged her shoulders. "My upbringing I guess. When you're raised Amish and your life turns out completely different, it's not easy to be close to anybody because they don't know who you are inside." She tapped on her heart with her fingers. "Do you understand that? Am I making any sense at all?"

"I think you're making perfect sense and I think you need to come back to the community."

Beverly giggled. "Do you?"

"Jah."

"I don't know about that. Everything's changed in my life now. That's why I was pleased to catch up with Leah. No one I met since I left has ever understood me, not really. On the outside, I look and sound like an *Englisch* woman, but deep down inside at the core of my being, I'm still Amish. I don't fit in anywhere." She wondered if God had called her back because that's where she was supposed to be. The community had been a safe place to grow up and, right up until her mother died, she had felt safe and loved.

"I think you don't get close to people because you don't relate to them, and if you don't relate to them, what are you doing out in the world when you should be back in the community?"

She stared into his eyes. "The problem is I don't agree with everything—all the Amish traditions and beliefs."

"You're probably over-thinking things. And if the things you don't agree with aren't big, why worry about them?" he asked.

"I don't know. It's not my life anymore."

"It could be."

"Anyway, how long were you with your girlfriend?"

"Only three months. I know that doesn't

sound like a long time... What about you? How long were you with your man?"

"Fifteen months. I met him at the bank."

"Was he your customer?"

Beverly giggled. "No, he was working at the bank. He's since moved on to work for another bank, thank goodness. I never have to see him and be reminded that he's married to somebody else."

"Love can be tough sometimes," he said in almost a whisper.

She probed further, wondering just how heartbroken he was over his broken relationship. "Did you think you were going to marry her?"

He nodded. "I had every intention of doing so and maybe that was the problem."

"How so?"

He smiled. "Maybe she read my thoughts because it was the very night I was going to ask her that she chose to end things between us."

They had both been hurt recently. Because of their similar backgrounds in their love lives, she felt close with him. "She didn't marry someone else though, did she?"

He smiled. "Not yet, but I suppose she will one day."

Beverly sighed. "It feels strange to be back here."

"You said this is the first time you've been back here since you were eighteen?"

"Yes, and that was ten years ago, and that means I'm twenty-eight if you're trying to work out my age."

"I wasn't. *Denke* for saving me doing the math."

"That's what I do best, after all."

"Good to know. I'll come looking for you if I ever need a loan. Anyway, I already figured out how old you were."

"How?"

"From how old you were when Janet and

Jeremiah married." His eyes crinkled at the corners.

"Ah." Beverly laughed. After they made their choice of a chest of drawers, they moved on to the nightstands.

"You and Leah would've had a lot of catching up to do," he said.

"It was so good to see her. It was funny to see her married and with four children. My other good friend is now married to Dora's son and they're living in Ohio. She's got two-year-old twin boys. I don't know if you've met Dora, but she does some cleaning for Janet."

"*Jah,* she was there this morning."

"That's right."

He sat himself down on a bed that was beside the nightstand she was looking at. "Did you always plan on leaving the community?"

"Nothing about my life has been planned. The answer is no. The only thing I planned were the courses I took in order to get a better job. I couldn't see myself working in fast food for the rest of my life. It was tiring being on my feet all day. And believe me, serving food is not as easy as it looks. I only worked there so I wouldn't have to rely on anybody else or call my father for money. I can just imagine how that conversation would've gone down. I couldn't have asked for money after I'd walked out." She bit her lip, unsure if he realized she'd only left after a huge row with Janet.

"Jeremiah's the only family you have?"

"I think my mother had cousins, but I don't know who they are or where they are. I've got relatives somewhere but I can't knock on the door ask them to help if I've never met them."

He chuckled. "I guess you're right, that would be strange."

"I've got friends."

"It's not the same."

Beverly knew he was right and wished her mother was still around. If *Mamm* hadn't died, she'd still be close with her father. It hadn't been entirely Janet's fault. He was a difficult man to get close to because he never spoke much. Her mother had told her many stories of what had happened when she was a little girl and her father never told her anything. When she was a teenager, she asked her father to tell her about his youth and he told her how he played cricket with his brothers on summer days and skated on frozen-over ponds in the winter. She never got told anything unless she asked.

"You've gone quiet."

"I was just thinking about my childhood."

"Reminiscing?"

"Yes. I've been doing a lot of that lately. Everything at home reminds me of my mother and that makes me sad. I used to get angry when people would say things were

God's will. Why was it God's will to take my mother away from me?"

"I don't think there's any answer. Except that we're not our own when we belong to God. We submit to Him and His will."

"Yes, there *is* an answer that people don't want to face."

He looked at her, shocked at her speaking out like that. "What do you mean?"

"Forget it."

"It's a little hard of you to say something like that and then not tell me what you mean. You can tell me what you mean, can't you? It's okay."

She looked into his eyes and believed he wouldn't pass judgement. "How could a loving God snatch a mother away from an only child?"

He slowly nodded. "And what is your answer, since you sound like you have one?"

"I don't think He's a loving God and my life proves that."

"Not one of us is guaranteed an easy life."

"I know that, but doesn't every child deserve a mother and father? If I'd never had a mother, I suppose I wouldn't have known her and then I wouldn't have missed her, but to give me a mother and take her away—words don't describe the feeling."

"I can't imagine."

She had never said her thoughts about this out loud, never shared them with anybody. It made her uneasy when he didn't respond. "I think that was cruel." She was expecting a reaction, and got none. "What do you think about that?"

"That's your opinion. You're entitled to it."

"I know it is and I asked you your opinion."

"When we're living on this earth we are humans and bound by earthly rules and earthly happenings and we're not fully spiritual beings as God is. When we pass on, and go to be with Him, we'll understand all things."

"You mean, I'll have to wait until I'm dead to know why my mother died?"

"That's right. And then you'll see her again."

She giggled because she didn't want to discuss religion, especially not in the furniture store. His reasoning was along the same lines as she'd heard preached so often. Beverly's relationship with God had become strained and uncertain ever since her mother died. Still, it had never occurred to her to leave the community until Janet drove her away with her unkindness. That's something she couldn't share with Janet's nephew, for sure. "I'm sorry, we've got all deep and meaningful and a little bit depressing."

"I don't mind talking about things like that. It's a nice change, and I like to hear what you think. Many people don't think deeply about things at all."

He looked at her and she turned to look at him and they smiled at one another.

"Well, have we made our choices?" She pointed to the chest of drawers. "Two of those and four of these." She tapped on the nightstand.

"Excellent choices." He leaped to his feet.

She rolled her eyes at him. "You'd would've said that about anything I chose."

"It's true, though." He grinned at her.

Beverly appreciated his calm nature. He was a man she could trust. She couldn't remember that she'd ever been able to tell anyone so much about herself. Especially all her deepest feelings, and when she had told him what was on her heart, there was no judgment.

THAT NIGHT as Beverly was falling asleep, she realized that God hadn't abandoned her just because she had left the community. He'd always been there, guiding her and watching over her, and He'd brought her safely home —maybe home to marry a wonderful man.

Then again, had she come all this way back to meet Oscar? They lived close, within streets of one another and worked close to each other. He'd be a good provider. He was the kind of man her friends were always saying she needed, but if he was all that, how could he still be single? And she was still concerned that he'd talked with Janet after she'd clearly requested he await her phone call.

CHAPTER 15

THAT EVENING, Beverly was delighted to go to Leah's house with David, and get away from those awkward dinners with Janet. She would also have a chance to meet Leah's older children. She wore a loose-fitting dress and flats in an effort not to offend anyone. Normally when she wasn't working, her go-to fashion item was a pair of jeans, but they just weren't acceptable around her Amish friends and family.

When Leah and Benjamin's house came into view, Beverly said, "Here we are."

"I can see I'm going to be spoiled while I'm here. With Janet's cooking and now out to dinner at Leah's *haus*."

"You know Leah's a good cook?"

"Any cooking would be better than mine," he joked.

"You live by yourself?"

"*Jah,* I'm a little too old to live with my folks."

"Did they kick you out?" Beverly knew that most Amish men lived at home until they married.

He chuckled. "It was close. I left when they were just about to, I think."

When he stopped the buggy, Beverly got out and waited for him to secure the horse. Just like a regular couple, they headed to the front door together. It was a simple thing, but Beverly liked how it felt to be part of a couple again.

Just as they were about to knock, Leah

opened the door. "Come in. It's lovely to see you again, David."

"And you," David said.

"Beverly, this is Benjamin."

Beverly reached out to shake his hand. He wasn't someone who'd grown up in this community, so he was new to her. "Nice to meet you."

He smiled at her. It was then she noticed that the three children were all lined up. "Oh, who do we have here?"

Leah said, "This is Amy, the oldest."

"I'm eight," Amy said.

Leah continued, "Sally is seven and Benjamin—"

Amy took over. "Benjamin is six. We call him Benny, so people don't think we're calling *Dat. Dat* and Benjamin have the same name."

"Children, this is Miss Beiler and Mr. Hilty."

"Hello," the three of them chorused.

"Now, go off and play and I'll call you when dinner's ready."

"Sally and I want to help, *Mamm,*" Amy said.

"Okay."

"Miss Beiler, the *boppli's* asleep."

"Is he? I saw him when I was here the other day."

David crouched down and spoke to Benjamin. "How about I play with you, Benny. Can you teach me some games?"

Benny nodded and the males made their way to the living room, while the girls went to the kitchen.

"The girls look so much like you, Leah. They've got your same light hair, and Benjamin is so much like his father."

"How do you know *Mamm?*" Amy asked.

Leah answered, "Beverly and I were friends since we were *bopplis.*"

Amy wrinkled her nose. "How can a *boppli* have a friend? *Bopplis* know nothing."

Beverly laughed. "We were friends since from as far back as we can remember."

"Why are you wearing funny clothes?" Sally asked Beverly.

"I'm not Amish anymore. I left a long time ago."

Sally looked her up and down. "Why?"

"It's a long story."

Leah stepped forward. *"Jah,* it's a long story and you won't be hearing it tonight."

"Ah, why not, *Mamm?* It's early. It's not even bedtime," Amy grumbled. "We haven't even had dinner."

Leah took on the typical mother's stance and wagged her finger. "Remember what I told both of you about adults talking?"

"Jah, we keep quiet," Sally said.

"Exactly. Now it's time for you girls to set the table."

The girls looked at one another with looks on their faces that said, there's no use, and then took handfuls of cutlery out of the drawer and began their chore of setting the table. Beverly stood there in wonderment as she watched them place the cutlery over the long wooden table. Ten years ago, they weren't there; now here they were large as life. Birth truly was a miracle and her friend had been blessed.

Leah distracted her thoughts when she whispered, "I'm sorry about that. Amy is a know-it-all. She's forever telling me a better way of doing things and she has trouble with listening."

"They're all so lovely—all your children."

Leah smiled. *"Denke.* Now tell me, how did you get away from Janet?"

"Yesterday, David let Janet know we were coming here for the evening meal. She didn't object."

"I was surprised to see both of you here tonight."

"You didn't think David would come?"

"I thought there was a chance he wouldn't. How's your *vadder?*"

"He's okay. I just learned he's planning on going to the meeting tomorrow, so he can't be too bad."

"That is good news."

"He'd probably crawl if he could. I don't think he ever missed one before his broken leg. I remember when I was a child, I had to be really, really sick before I could stay at home."

She noticed Leah was distracted, too busy stirring something on the stove. "What can I do to help?"

"There's really not much you can do except talk to me."

She looked over at Leah's girls and wondered what it would be like to have four children; she didn't think she'd be able to handle so many. Every time she thought back on her childhood, Janet's austere face kept jumping into her mind. Her father seemed happy with Janet, though.

Beverly didn't need to ask her friend if she was happy with her life because she could tell from just being around her that she was. She was contented looking after home and husband and four children, and if she was anything like most of the other Amish women, she'd go on to have a lot more children. The life Beverly had in New York City now seemed so far away.

Maybe God did have His hand on her after all. He brought her back to the Amish to marry David. She giggled at the silly thoughts in her head until it struck her that it might be true. Even though she didn't agree with many of the Amish traditions, from being out in the world, she could see that the basic principles were good. The children were protected from the horrible things in society, and without electricity there were no video games or television, and the family unit stayed intact.

She'd always seen herself with a man like David, but was he attracted to her? Or did he think of her as just a friend? Maybe it had been a mistake to tell him all those things about herself. On the other hand, they got along really well and she had never found someone with whom she could talk so easily. She closed her eyes and couldn't help smiling when she imagined herself back in the community and married to David, with one, or maybe two, children. She'd be an older mother just like her mother before her had been, but that was okay. She couldn't change that fact. Once she married, gone would be the pressure of her job and having to make the quotas just to maintain her position. As much as she loved her job she didn't like the continual pressure that came with it.

For dinner, the children had their own small table to sit at next to the adults and weren't allowed to speak with the adults during dinner.

In the midst of the dinner, Beverly announced, "A man has come out of nowhere and wants to buy the bed-and-breakfast,"

"What man?" Leah asked.

"He's a lawyer from the city. He grew up around here and wants it as a vacation home."

"He must have a large family," Benjamin said.

"He's single."

Benjamin leaned forward. "Hang on a minute. His name's not Oscar something or other, is it?"

Beverly braced herself to hear some particularly bad news. "Yes, Oscar Reynolds."

"That's it, Reynolds. I've heard of him. He's got a client who buys up land that has caves on it containing archaeological things. In the valley, they've found some large skeletons and some say it's proof giants used to live around here."

Beverly gasped. "Leah, there's a cave on the property. We used to play in it as children, remember?"

"That's right. We were too scared to go too far inside; it seemed like it went on forever. For as far as we could see."

"What if this man knows there's something worthwhile in those caves? Something of value? Is that why he wants to buy the place?" David asked.

"It's sounds possible," Benjamin said. "There were other various artifacts found, and old jewelry. This man, I don't know who he was, but Reynolds was doing the deal—he made an offer and people sold to him, and then regretted it when they found out what they'd sold."

"I remember something about that now. I knew nothing about it when I was living here, but a couple of years ago I was bored and I looked up the history of the Conewango Valley. It never occurred to me that there might be something in that cave until right now."

"Janet and Jeremiah's problems might be over if something comes of this." David's face beamed.

Beverly nodded. "That's right. People will want to come to the land to see the cave. Maybe if there are skeletons, they would be worth some money to a museum or something. I guess we'd donate them, but think of all the publicity that would be generated from such a discovery." When she saw everyone at the table was looking at her, she giggled. "I'm getting carried away. I always do that."

"Let's go there at first light, Beverly." David said.

Beverly looked at him to see that he was just as excited. "Okay. Um, there's always the chance that the lawyer's telling the truth and he just wants the place for vacations."

Benjamin said, "I'd help, but I promised to help my brother early tomorrow morning."

"*Jah,* and I've got the *kinner,*" Leah said. "Otherwise, I'd come too."

"We'll let you know what we find," Beverly said, wishing it was daylight right now.

"We'll need flashlights," David said.

"We've got them back at the house." Beverly said.

Leah moved in her seat. "Now I can't wait. Be sure to tell us the moment you find anything."

Beverly giggled. "I will."

"*Mamm,* can we have dessert?" Amy asked. "We've all finished."

"What did I tell you about sitting quietly and waiting for dessert when we have visitors?" Leah glared at Amy.

"Sorry, *Mamm.*"

"Yah, sorry, *Mamm,*" the younger sister repeated while Benny banged his fork on the table.

Leah leaped up and promptly took the fork from him, which made him cry.

"Sounds like someone is ready for bed," Benjamin said.

Benny whined, *"Nee, Dat."*

"Well, stop crying if you want dessert." Leah turned back around. "I'm sorry, but they're not usually like this. They're usually so well-behaved."

"Perhaps they want attention," David said.

"They're getting attention all right, but not the right kind of attention," Benjamin said. "I guess we should have dinner guests more often so they get more practice."

Beverly had never felt so at home with people, not in such a long time. After the children went to bed, the four adults sat there enjoying the conversation like two married couples. It gave Beverly a taste of what could be in her future.

When there was a lull in the conversation Beverly said, "It's getting quite late. We better be on our way and let you two get some sleep."

David stood up. "Thank you both for a lovely dinner."

"Thank you for sparing some of your time to join us tonight. I know you don't have a lot of time here."

"When are you going back?" Benjamin asked David.

"I'm not too sure. I'm playing it by ear. I think Beverly's got a lot of jobs for me to finish before I leave." He chuckled.

Beverly liked the way he was referring to her; it was like they were a couple for real. As the four of them walked to the buggy, Beverly's thoughts turned back to the coming morning and the conversation about the traces that might be hidden in the cave.

"I think it's silly to hope that there are valuable relics in the cave."

David laughed at her.

"What did I say?" Beverly asked.

"You're excited about what we'll find tomorrow morning."

"Aren't you?"

"I must admit I am."

"I'm glad I'm not the only one. I just don't want to get my hopes up. I mean, it's just a cave."

"An unexplored cave by the sounds of it," Benjamin said.

"I don't know. Just unexplored by me and my friends. The previous owners of the property would've known the cave was there, so maybe they checked it out."

"We don't have long to wait to find out. We can go there at first light, or do you want to go there tonight?"

Beverly shuddered. "No way. There's no

way I'd go there tonight. It'd be far too scary."

David chuckled, along with Benjamin and Leah. "At first light, then," he said.

"Can we get away without Janet knowing what we're doing?"

"What would it matter if she knew?" Leah asked.

"I don't know. I think she'll think it just sounds kind of silly."

"What does it matter? Are you really worried if Janet thinks we're silly?" David tilted his head and gave her a cheeky grin.

Beverly giggled. "I'm sure she already thinks I'm silly."

"There you go, you've got nothing further to worry about then."

Everyone chuckled. David always said things to comfort her and make her feel better.

· · ·

LATER THAT NIGHT when they got back to the house, Beverly offered to help him with the horse and buggy.

"Go inside and I'll meet you in the kitchen as soon as the sun's up. And find those flashlights."

"Okay. I had a really good time tonight."

He smiled at her and, in the moonlight, she saw his eyes crinkle around the corners. "Me too."

She turned away from him and headed to the house. When she opened the door, she saw that everything was quiet and still and there was no sign of Janet. She lit the small lantern, turned off the overhead gaslight and then made her way up the stairs. This was the best she'd felt in years. When she'd been with Kevin, she never truly felt good about herself. David made her feel the opposite. Then there was Oscar. There was a man she'd like to learn a lot more about. Although... She hoped he didn't have an ulterior motive for wanting to buy the property. David might've been right. Oscar might know there was something valuable on the land.

After a quick shower, she changed into a soft over-sized t-shirt and slipped between the sheets. Tossing and turning instead of dozing off, she soon realized she was going to get little sleep. Her adrenaline levels were high with excitement about what they might find the next day. Then she couldn't help wondering what her life would be like if she married David.

Hours later, Beverly was finally drifting off to sleep when she heard the first sounds of birds, signaling the predawn. Even though she knew it meant she'd soon have to get out of bed and her chances of sleep were gone, she appreciated their beautiful sounds. She never heard those sounds in the city.

CHAPTER 16

WHEN IT GOT BRIGHTER OUTSIDE, Beverly forced herself out of bed, got changed and made herself presentable before she headed downstairs.

Janet and David were sitting at the table and they both turned to look at her.

Janet asked, "Do you think there's anything in the cave?"

"David told you about the cave?"

"*Jah.*"

She glanced over at David. "I suppose

there's a chance. It's worth checking out, I think."

"What a good idea."

Beverly was shocked to hear that. She never would've thought Janet would approve of them looking in the cave.

"Coffee?" David asked her.

"Yes please." She pulled out a high-backed wooden chair and sat down at the kitchen table. The table and chairs were the same ones that had always been there. "I don't think I had any sleep. I was too excited about what we might find today."

He poured the coffee, and then placed it in front of her. "I didn't have a problem. I always fall asleep as soon as my head hits the pillow."

She groaned as she took the coffee. "I wish I could do that. My mind always takes a while to shut down. Thanks for this." She blew on it and then took a sip.

"Do you want breakfast before you head out?" Janet asked.

"*Nee.* We'll have some when we come back if that's alright, Aunt Janet."

"That's quite all right. I've got those flashlights for you too."

Janet went into the utility room, pulled out the flashlights and placed them on the table.

"I'll just finish this and then I'll be ready to go."

Janet was flitting about the kitchen. It seemed she was excited about what they might find.

"There might not be anything there, Janet. I never saw anything there when I played in the caves with my friends."

"That might have been because you weren't looking."

"We would've noticed. But we didn't ever go the full way inside. It was too dark and scary."

"You'll soon find out."

"Don't be disappointed if there's nothing there."

"I won't."

"Good." Beverly took another swallow of coffee and then she and David headed out of the house and make their way through the long grass. "We really must get someone in to restore the garden and fix up these yards. They look a fright."

"Are they going to go ahead with the loan, or what?" David asked.

"I'll try to get an answer from my father today. He sounded more open after I met with the loan officer at the bank, and so did Janet. They really need to make some decisions so we know what direction we're heading with everything."

"Maybe we'll find something in those caves and their decision will be made easier."

Beverly nodded. "I hope so."

They soon came to the entrance of the

cave, but it had grown over with brambles and tangled vines. "It's right here."

"Are you sure?"

"I am. No one's been here in years."

"I'm not so sure about that." David leaned down and picked something out of the grass. It was a cigarette butt. He threw it back down and then he pulled on the greenery covering the cave and it came away in one piece, almost like a gate.

"Someone's been here, and they deliberately camouflaged the opening of this cave. Recently, too, or that cigarette butt would have begun to disintegrate."

"Yes. They tried to cover their tracks."

He moved the mat of interwoven greenery off to the side and then flipped on his flashlight. "After you."

She looked up to see him smirking. "No way, after you."

He laughed. "You can stay there if you want to. You don't have to come with me."

"I'll come too, but I just don't want to go first."

He made his way into the cave and shone his flashlight on the ground. "Footprints, and there are a few of them."

Beverly leaned over and made out at least three different types of shoe prints. "Now we know someone's been here for sure. More than one someone."

They continued forward about twenty feet until the cavern ended.

"Is this all?" she asked, shining her flashlight on the walls and hoping to find some cave paintings or such.

"*Nee.* Look over there; it continues, but it gets narrower. Too narrow for me to move through. You could probably fit in it."

Beverly shined her flashlight where David's was focused, and found the opening to the other section of the cave. "I'm not going to. I tend to get claustrophobic in small spaces. I'm doing all right so far, but there's no way I would go in there."

"Well, that's it then. I can't see anything of interest. Shall we turn around and go?"

"Yes." On the way out, Beverly moved her flashlight carefully around, hoping to see something interesting. Once they were out into the morning daylight, Beverly brushed herself down. "That was disappointing. I'm still curious about how much farther it goes - there could be branches off that smaller area. What if there was treasure and now it's been taken?"

"It's possible. Or someone might have come just to shelter themselves. A homeless person perhaps? Well, several, given the different shoe-print patterns."

"That's possible too. Someone got creative, making that mat of vines and branches to cover the opening."

He started walking, and she fell in beside him.

"I guess that's all we can do," he said, "unless we find someone brave enough to go into that small cave. Maybe a couple smaller teenage boys..."

"Maybe, but it could be dangerous. We'll need to be more alert for trespassers on the property."

He nodded. "True. And we'll have to give Janet the bad news."

Switching off her flashlight, she said, "You should do that since you're her nephew."

He chuckled. "You're the stepdaughter."

She crinkled her nose. "I think you're just reinforcing my point."

As they walked back to the house, Beverly couldn't help being a little disappointed that they had found nothing there, at least for Janet and Jeremiah's sake. She was more determined than ever to push Jeremiah into making a decision.

LATER THAT DAY, Beverly sat on the edge of her father's bed.

"There was no treasure?"

She saw amusement on his face and knew he wasn't too disappointed about there not being any relics in the cave. "Oh, Janet told you?"

"She tells me everything."

"No, there was no treasure. None that we were able to find, anyway, and if there was anything it's gone now. It's important that you make a decision. Stay here and make the place work, or sell. Which one is it going to be?"

He chuckled. "You're determined, just like your *mudder*."

"I take that as a compliment. Which one, *Dat*? I have to know because I'll find some influential people who can help and invite them to the relaunch if you decide to stay. If you want to sell, I'll help organize that."

"I've talked to Janet and we've decided we don't want to sell. We enjoy having people stay here. We get to know people from all over the country."

"That is settled then, but then you'll need to agree to a loan."

"*Jah*, we'll get the loan. We'll go ahead with that. We trust that you know what you're doing."

"Good; finally. I'll call the bank today and tell them that we're going ahead with a loan. They'll send out some papers that you will need to sign."

"We'll do whatever we have to."

"We'll set up an account at the hardware store so we can buy paints and things like that."

"Don't go crazy. We've got tools in the barn. Don't double up."

"Okay, I won't. Don't worry."

"Very good."

"I think it'll only take about a week to whip this place into shape. We must get started on the painting today, and then I'll make some arrangements to have a big re-opening launch party."

"Do whatever you need to do. Janet and I will do whatever you say."

Beverly nodded, pleased that they both trusted her.

She headed back down the stairs, elated that her father had made a good decision. She found David in the kitchen finishing off his breakfast. She didn't know where Janet was, and she was pleased to be able to talk with David in private. "Jeremiah agreed to take out a loan."

"That's great news."

"I know. Are you free today to help me with some painting?"

"Of course. Inside or outside?"

"Inside to start with. Do we really need to

paint outside? Would it be okay with just a cleaning?"

"I'll have a better look at it as soon as I finish breakfast."

"Then can you take me to buy the paint?"

"I'm here to do whatever you need me to do."

Beverly smiled. "Thank you."

"Are you coming to the meeting with us tomorrow?"

Beverly nearly choked. "Meeting? Is there really a meeting tomorrow?"

"That's right. Remember? We talked about it at Leah's."

"Someone should stay and look after *Dat.*"

"I believe he's going to the meeting."

"Really? Oh yes, I do remember hearing something about that, but I didn't think he was serious. He can barely walk."

"He wants to go."

"I don't think anyone wants to see me."

"Don't you want to go?"

Beverly thought about it for a while before she answered. She didn't want to go and she was avoiding telling him outright. "I wouldn't be comfortable."

"Fair enough."

Beverly grimaced. "I wouldn't like everyone looking at me, and all the questions."

"I can understand that."

CHAPTER 17

THE NEXT DAY WAS SUNDAY, and when Beverly woke she found herself alone in the house. She'd slept in after her sleepless night the night before, which had been followed by the cave outing and a huge afternoon of painting. She been so fast asleep that she hadn't even heard them all leave.

Realizing no one was going to be about, she changed into her favorite jeans and a t-shirt, and then headed downstairs for a breakfast of coffee and toast. When she got there, there was no bread. There was only a stale old scrap of bread in the bread bin. She tossed it back in disgust and headed for the coffee pot. It wasn't great coffee, not like the coffee from her electric brewer in her apartment, but it was better than instant.

While she sat and drank her coffee, she couldn't get it out of her mind how Oscar had come there when she'd told him she was handling it. The more she thought about it, the more it infuriated her. She made up her mind then and there to call him and give him a piece of her mind.

After she found his business card, she marched to the phone in the barn. Once she was in the barn, she did her best to ignore the mess. It was another thing that had to be cleaned and organized.

She took a long deep breath, exhaling slowly as she rehearsed everything she wanted to say, and then dialed his number. Oscar answered after two rings, sounding like he'd just woken up.

"Hello?"

"Hi Oscar, it's Beverly Beiler."

"Oh, Beverly. I didn't recognize the number. Don't you have a cell phone?"

"I do, but it's not charged. No electricity here, remember? The reason I'm calling is that I'm quite shocked that you came here the other day and spoke to my stepmother on her own." She was pleased she'd spoken her mind, but anxious when there was a long pause.

He finally said, "What's got you so hot and bothered?"

"I told you I'd handle it, to wait for my call."

"Beverly, there was no harm done. Janet and I had a nice talk."

"I told you I was handling things," she repeated. "I don't want them being harassed. They're both old."

"Forgive me. I was too impatient. There was no harm done was there?"

"I suppose there wasn't, but can you leave things with me? I don't like them to be under any pressure."

"I understand. I'll leave things with you from now on. Okay?"

"Good. Thank you." She was pleased she'd called him.

"Did Janet tell you I made her an offer?"

"She did and they're still deciding what to do." She didn't want to reveal their decision just yet in case they ended up needing to sell.

"And you're helping them, I hope?"

"All I'm doing is helping them to make the right decision. The right decision for them."

"Look, I'm truly sorry. I can tell you're upset. How about we talk about this further later today? Over lunch, or breakfast?"

Hmm, breakfast. She thought about the stale scrap of bread, which seemed to be the only food at hand. There was never much food on a Sunday, the day of rest. "Breakfast sounds good."

"Breakfast it is, then."

"Can you collect me? They've taken the only buggy to their meeting."

"Left you home alone, have they?"

"Yes."

"Give me fifteen." He ended the call.

She looked down at what she was wearing. The skinny jeans were okay and she'd exchange the t-shirt for a blouse. And, she'd have to put makeup on if she was going to be out in civilization.

WHEN OSCAR ARRIVED at the house, she was ready and waiting with a freshly made up face and heels. Janet didn't appreciate her wearing jeans, as the Amish regarded jeans or pants as men's clothing and not appropriate for a woman to wear. She'd change into a skirt if she arrived back home before Janet.

He jumped out of his car as soon as it stopped and hurried to open the passenger door. "Your carriage awaits."

"It's a funny looking carriage." She slid into the front seat.

"Only the best." He closed the door and got in beside her. Gone was the suit. He wore light-colored pants and a pale blue shirt, which enhanced his tanned skin and made his eyes even bluer.

He looked at her and smiled. "You look lovely today."

"Thank you."

"I'm taking you to my favorite breakfast place."

"Sounds good. I'm a little hungry."

"You won't be disappointed. Don't be fooled by the exterior of the place. It's not much to look at, but the food's amazing."

. . .

THEY SAT in the booth of the diner and, after they'd ordered, the waitress poured them both coffee.

Beverly looked up at her and smiled. "Thank you." Then Beverly looked back at Oscar who was staring at her. She couldn't lead him on about the place. When the waitress left, Beverly blurted out, "I didn't tell you this on the phone, sorry, but they're not selling now."

His face fell. "Beverly, you were supposed to be on my side."

"I have to be on *their* side. It's their decision."

"You said they were getting old and should sell."

"They're not that old."

"Janet tells me your father's in his eighties."

"Yes, but apart from his broken leg he's never had a day's sickness in his life. And once they get people staying there again, the maintenance won't be such a problem. My father won't have to do everything himself."

"I have to tell you I'm disappointed. I had my heart set on the place. Do you think they'll sell in the future?"

Visions of the footprints in the cave, and the cigarette butt they'd found at the entrance, jumped into her mind. "Are you sure it was just the property you were interested in?"

He chuckled. "You caught me out. At the start, it was all about the property, but then I saw you. Is there any chance we could have dinner when we're both back in the city?"

"Oh, I didn't mean me."

His eyebrows pinched together. "Who did you mean then?"

She shook her head. "I mean were you interested in the house alone? Was there something, anything, you're keeping from me about why you're so interested?"

The waitress interrupted them as she

placed their meals in front of them. Both of them had ordered the large breakfast, which consisted of bacon and eggs with hash browns and toast.

Oscar thanked the waitress as she left. "Beverly, what are you trying to say? I'm not a liar." He picked up his knife and fork. "I told you and Janet from the beginning that I'm not out to defraud you. I'm willing to pay above the going rate for the property, and I still am."

"That's not what I meant." She looked down at the huge meal in front of her. "Don't worry."

He set about eating, and she did the same. Beverly told herself that just because someone had been in the cave it didn't mean that Oscar had been the one, or that he knew about it. In an effort to make it up to him, she asked, "Would you like to come to the relaunch party after we give the place a makeover?"

"Is that what you're doing?"

She nodded. "We're giving the house a makeover and having a party to attract some interest."

"I'll come. Thank you. That'll give me a chance to get inside the place and have a look at least. Janet wouldn't let me see beyond the living room. When is it?"

"We don't have a date set down for it yet. It'll be in a week or two, maybe three. I'll call you."

At that moment, his cell phone rang and he pulled it out of his pocket. He looked up at her and gave her a wink. "I'll be waiting. Excuse me." He got up and stepped away from the table to answer the phone.

An hour and a half later, she was back at the house. She quickly changed out of her jeans and back into a skirt, and then decided to start cleaning more of the walls to get them ready for painting. Since the Amish didn't work on Sunday, David wouldn't be able to help when he got back home, and she was anxious to keep up the momentum they'd started the previous day.

It was late in the afternoon when David, Janet and Jeremiah arrived home. Her father was exhausted and went upstairs to bed. David seemed distant. It might have been because Janet was excitedly jabbering away about the new quilts she'd ordered from her friend. Janet was so excited that Beverly didn't even ask how much they were. If the frugal Janet had ordered them, they must have been a reasonable price.

CHAPTER 18

ON MONDAY, after they moved all the furniture out of the way and into another of the bedrooms, David poured the paint into a tray.

"Did everything go okay at the meeting yesterday?"

He looked up at her. *"Jah.* Why?"

"You seemed kind of strange when you came back here."

"In what way?"

"Just not yourself."

"I've had a lot on my mind."

Beverly wondered if he'd been thinking about her. "Like what?"

"Nothing that you'd be interested in. Do you want the roller and I'll do the edges like we did on Saturday?"

"Yes. I'll take the easiest job—the roller."

"Have you painted much before?"

"Yes. I helped Janet paint the place many years ago now."

"From the looks of the walls, I'd say it was a long time ago."

Beverly giggled. "It will make such a difference when they're done."

They painted in silence for some time, until David said, "Are you really leaving here, Beverly? For some reason, most likely just a selfish reason, I had hoped you might consider staying."

She stared at him. Was he going to give her a reason to stay? "You know I don't agree with all the beliefs."

"I know, but do you have to agree with

everything as long as you believe in the basic principles and want to spend eternity with our Lord and Savior?"

Was he in love with her, or was he just trying to save her soul? "I can't give you an answer. Who knows what the future might bring?"

"We shape our future by our daily decisions."

"I guess that's true up to a point, but everything's not up to us. We could make plans and then something unpredictable happens that's beyond our control." She thought back to Kevin and how she might have been married to him by now if he hadn't suddenly dumped her. There was nothing she could've done about that because it wasn't up to her in the end.

"We're all subject to *Gott's* will and what He wants for our life."

"I know all about that."

"Me too."

"I made some weird decisions. I never got over losing my mother and I don't think it's something I will ever get over. For a long time, I thought it was simply time that would heal me, but it didn't. When I left, I chose to live in the Harlem area. Back then it was cheap, which was convenient, but it wasn't the best place to live—not the part of it I was in. I was rebelling from the community. I wanted to embrace the *Englisch* world."

"Weren't you worried it was dangerous?"

"The only danger I feared back then was living a life of boredom. If I was in danger, it meant at least I was alive."

He took the small brush and dipped it into the paint. As he smoothed the paint along the sides of the corners, he asked, "What do you want out of life?"

"What everyone wants—to be happy."

"What is happiness for you?"

She smoothed the roller up and down the wall. "I want a family."

"Children?"

"Yes."

"Lots of them?"

She giggled. "I don't know. I've left my run a bit too late to have too many. I'd like one or two, or at the most three. My mother didn't have me until she was in her forties. They couldn't have children, or thought they couldn't, I should say, because it had never happened for them and all of a sudden when they'd given up, I showed up."

He turned around and loaded the brush with more paint. "I can imagine how delighted they were to find out you were on the way."

"*Jah*, they were and they never had any more, just me." She giggled. "*Dat* used to joke that I was so much trouble that I made up for a houseful of *kinner*."

"A bit naughty, were you?"

"No. But I was a little stubborn when I got older. What about you?"

"I lost my parents at a young age."

"Both of them?"

"Jah."

"I'm sorry, I didn't know."

"I don't go around telling everyone."

"That must've been hard."

"It was, but we all adapted."

"How did they die?"

"My mother drowned. She caught her legs in reeds and my father tried to drag her out, but he couldn't. He died a week later of pneumonia."

"That's so sad. You weren't there to witness it, were you?"

"Thankfully we weren't. We were cooking a surprise meal for our mother. She hadn't been well and we were doing something nice for her. We had *Dat* take her out of the house so she wouldn't see what we were doing. It was a Saturday, a hot summer Saturday and they decided to go for a swim. She left her long dress on and it became entangled when she dove into the water."

Beverly swallowed hard. Here she was moaning about God taking away her mother when he'd lost both of his parents. "I'm so sorry to hear that, David. I also lost my mother to pneumonia, but to lose both parents is awful. I don't know how you carried on."

"We managed. We were split in pairs and sent to live with relatives. There were six of us, so we went to three different *onkels* and aunts."

"I remember you said your parents had both come from families of twelve."

"*Jah.* I went with my younger *bruder* by one year, Peter. He died eighteen months after that from leukaemia."

No longer could Beverly hold back her tears. She placed the roller down and in an effort to conceal the fact she was crying she turned her body to look out the window.

"Beverly."

"*Jah.*"

"I'm sorry, I didn't mean to upset you. It's something I don't normally tell people, but I thought ..."

"It's okay." She sniffed and heard him set down his brush and walk toward her. She felt warm hands laid gently on her shoulders. Still looking out the window she said, "You should've said something when I told you about my *mudder.*"

"*Nee.* You needed to tell me your story right then, without being burdened with mine. Your loss is painful and so is my loss, but we can't let that rule our lives. Our lives belong to *Gott* to do what He wants. We are not our own."

"I don't know if I can accept that."

Gently, he turned her around to face him. "What choice do we have, Beverly? Even if you're an unbeliever and don't accept that everything is in *Gott's* plan, isn't it better to accept what has happened? It's already done and nothing you and I can do or say will bring our loved ones back. For your own peace of mind, isn't it best to accept?"

She stared into his eyes. "Yes, you're right."

His eyes moved from her eyes to her mouth, his hands moved from her arms to the hollow of her back as he slowly pulled her toward him. Beverly knew this was the moment she'd been waiting for. Everything in her life had been leading up to this point.

Closing her eyes, she slowly parted her lips and just as she felt his lips touch hers, the handle of the closed door creaked and they jumped apart.

It was Janet. She stood in the doorway staring back and forth between the two of them.

"David, would you mind driving me into town?"

He looked over at Beverly and then

looked back at Janet. "Isn't it best that I stay here and paint? There's a lot to do."

"Eli has told me that there are four young men in the community willing to paint the house. That will relieve both of you from doing the work. You can supervise them, Beverly."

"Sounds good." Beverly forced a smile. It was just like Janet to ruin everything. If she hadn't barged in, they would've kissed and then they would both have to admit that they liked one another.

"You want to go now, Janet?" he asked.

"*Jah*, now. Unless there's a reason you don't want to."

"*Nee,* that's fine."

"You go, David. I'll finish painting this room. When are the boys coming Janet?"

"I've just got word they're coming later today."

"Good. With four of them the place will be painted in no time."

Janet stood there waiting for David to leave with her, then and there. She was obviously not going to give them even a moment alone.

It was several minutes after Janet and David had left in the buggy that Beverly heard knocking. Someone was knocking on the front door.

She opened the door to see a young Amish woman. "Hello." Beverly figured she might be the daughter of one of Janet's friends.

"I was told David Hilty is staying here."

"Yes, he is, but he's not here at the moment." The woman looked troubled. "Would you like to come in and wait for him?"

"Would you mind?"

"Of course not. Come in."

Beverly guessed now that this was the girlfriend that had upset David so much by choosing another man over him. It looked like she'd changed her mind and was running back to him. And who could blame her? She obviously realised what she had let go of.

When the young woman had walked inside, Beverly said, "I'm Jeremiah's daughter." The woman didn't register any knowledge of who Jeremiah was. Beverly continued, "Jeremiah owns this place."

"Oh, that's right, and Jeremiah is married to David's aunt?"

"Yes. Would you like a cup of tea?"

The woman smiled. "I would love one, *denke*."

She walked with the woman into the kitchen. "Did David know you were coming?"

"No. It was a last-minute thing. I mean, it was a last-minute decision to come here."

Beverly filled the teakettle and then lit the gas stove before she placed the kettle atop the flame. She then filled a plate with cookies from the jar.

"Denke," the young woman said as she reached out and took a cookie.

Beverly sat opposite her trying to think of something to say.

"Where is David now?" the young woman asked.

"He's just gone to town with his aunt, to help her with an errand."

"Do you live here?" she asked.

"No, I'm just visiting. I live in New York City. And where are you from?"

"I'm from Walnut Creek."

Beverly nodded, remembering that David was also from Walnut Creek. That confirmed it; this woman was David's ex-girlfriend running back to him. "That's quite a long way from here."

"I know."

"I'm Beverly Beiler."

"I'm Susan King."

Beverly smiled politely, hiding her disappointment. She had no other choice.

CHAPTER 19

WHEN JANET ARRIVED HOME, Beverly quickly
introduced Susan to her while David was
still outdoors taking care of the horse and
buggy, and then she headed to her room to
avoid witnessing the reunion between Susan
and David. When she heard a buggy arriving
a bit later, she looked out the window. It was
Irma, the bishop's wife. From the safety of
her upstairs room, she watched as David ac-
companied Susan to the buggy. Putting two
and two together, Beverly figured Janet had

asked Irma if Susan could stay with her and Eli.

It made Beverly feel better to see Susan leaving in that buggy. Sooner or later, she'd have to go down the stairs and face David.

Fifteen minutes later, Beverly headed down the stairs and was just about to walk into the kitchen when she heard David and Janet talking.

"When will the wedding be?" Janet asked.

"I'm not sure."

"But you are going to marry her?" Janet asked.

He replied, "Yes."

Beverly had her answer. She walked into the kitchen and from the look on David's face, he knew she had overheard enough...

"Congratulations, David," Beverly said.

He swallowed hard and then nodded.

Beverly looked over at Janet. "Susan's gone?"

Janet said, "I thought it best she stayed elsewhere."

"When are you leaving, David?"

"Soon. I thought it best I leave the day after tomorrow."

"You mean 'we,' don't you?" Janet asked him.

"*Jah.* Of course. Susan and I."

The only thing Beverly could do was act as though it didn't bother her. "You'll miss the relaunch."

"I know and I'm sorry."

"Thanks for all your help. I couldn't have done so much without you."

His lips curved upwards into a smile. "I was happy to help. I've enjoyed my stay here."

"It's a shame it wasn't for longer," Janet said.

Beverly stared at Janet, wishing she would leave so she could have a quiet moment alone with David. Janet didn't take the hint, or didn't want to leave them alone. Either way, Beverly was going to have to wait until the next night to be alone with him, and that was his last night there.

Jeremiah had made it downstairs to have dinner in honor of David's last night. They had a meal of roast turkey with Janet's breaded stuffing that she made so well. There were also the vegetables that Janet loved the most, green beans, corn on the cob, and mashed potatoes. For dessert, they had chocolate pie with ice cream and Janet's much-loved chocolate covered salted caramel sweets.

When the dinner was over, Janet helped Jeremiah back upstairs while Beverly and David sat alone in the living room.

David was the first to speak. "I'm sorry things worked out like this."

Beverly couldn't look at him and had

barely said a word throughout the dinner. Even though she'd been waiting for a moment alone with him, there was nothing she could say. He had chosen Susan—a woman who had already rejected him—so there was no more to be said. The only thing she could do was try to talk him out of marrying Susan, but no, she wanted a man who chose her.

"I would've liked to be here for the party and to have stayed and seen it through."

"I know, but now you've got Susan."

"*Jah.*"

"And the two of you will marry."

"Well, we had planned to and now—"

"I'm happy for you."

"I need to tell you—"

"No. Nothing needs to be said and I'll need to sleep a lot to be ready for tomorrow. I'm very tired. I haven't been myself lately, so I'll say goodbye now."

He nodded.

She stood up. "Goodbye, David Hilty. It was lovely to meet you." When he stood, she nearly offered her hand for him to shake, but she couldn't bear to feel his touch not after the kiss they had just barely shared.

"Goodbye, Beverly."

She rushed away and headed up the stairs. All the way, she felt him watching her. Once she was in the safety of her room, she closed the door behind her. If there was one thing Beverly didn't like, it was this feeling of emptiness in her heart. She loved her father, but he chose Janet over her, and now David had chosen Susan. When was someone going to choose her?

All she wanted was to be loved. Couldn't she have someone who couldn't bear to be without her? Closing her eyes, she slumped onto the bed, and she did something she'd done so many times before. She prayed to God, asking Him to bring her that one special man, the man who would love her and look after her. The thing she struggled with was her wavering faith. God rewarded faith and answered the prayers of the faithful; those who firmly believed their prayers would be answered. It was hard for Beverly to have faith enough to believe her life could change.

FOR THE NEXT few days after David left, Beverly kept herself busy supervising the people who were helping to fix the house and the gardens. To keep her mind off David, she thought more about Oscar. After all, Oscar was available and David wasn't. It certainly made more sense in some ways to be with a man like Oscar, since she'd be heading back to New York soon enough.

One thing she knew for certain; she couldn't wait to get back home to her normal life. And it seemed Oscar would fit into her life so well. He was perfect boyfriend material.

"WE HAVE THE FINAL NUMBERS, Janet. There'll be eighty-three people coming."

Janet's thin mouth turned down at the corners. "Is that all?"

"That's all we need. There are travel bloggers, people from the tourist industry, people from travel magazines, and from the local newspaper. If we impress them, they'll reach thousands of people and then we'll get a lot of bookings—all the bookings you can handle."

When she saw a tiny smile appear on Janet's face, that made Beverly happy.

"And what will I be cooking for all these people?"

"I was thinking finger food—no big meals or anything. Just some quick light tasty morsels of food."

Janet's face beamed. "I can do that."

"And I can help too."

"Good," Janet said. "The rooms look good. *Denke* for doing everything so quickly and I hope this makes a difference."

"You're welcome. I think that's why *Dat's* getting around better. He wants to be at that party talking to people."

Janet chuckled. "He does like to talk."

Beverly was pleased by how much more pleasant Janet had become now that the weight of stress was lifting.

THE EVENING of the relaunch party rolled around.

Lights and lanterns hung close to the house in the tree branches, making the place look like a wonderland.

Large trestle tables of food were set up,

holding bite-sized samples of many of the foods typically served at the bed-and-breakfast. The house was open for inspection by the guests, who were encouraged to take a plate of food with them and wander around the guest quarters and living areas.

Beverly was pleased to see her father talking to as many people as he could, and Janet was creating smiles on the faces of the people she was talking with.

After Beverly chatted with a few people, she made her way to Oscar, who had been sitting down on one of the benches under the trees outside.

"So, I finally get to talk to you."

She giggled. "It is a big night for my father and Janet. Have you looked through the house?"

"I have and I still want to buy it. I'll go beyond the original offer I gave Janet." He rubbed his neck. "I thought that was a reasonable offer, but she didn't seem impressed."

"They're not selling. Not now."

"You said they might have to if this place doesn't work."

"I think it will work, after tonight. Everyone seems impressed."

"Good for you, but not so good for me. Anyway, when we get back to the city, how about dinner?" When she took too long to answer, he added, "Are you going to make me work hard for that too?"

She shook her head.

"Is that a no, meaning no you're not going to make me work hard for it?"

There was one thing standing in Beverly's way of going on a date with Oscar and that was the nagging doubts she still had about him. She figured honesty was the best policy. "When I was having dinner at my friend's house... Well, the thing is, I've heard about how you're working with a client of yours to buy property in the valley, cheaply."

"Cheaply? I said I'll offer a good price and I don't have a client wanting me to buy it on their behalf. It's just me."

"My friend said—"

"Your friend's crazy."

"Okay. Not crazy, but maybe mis-informed."

"Tell me exactly what she said, or was it a he?"

"Um, it was the husband of my friend. He heard somewhere about you wanting to buy other people's land in this area for rare ar-tifacts."

His eyes opened wide. "What did you hear exactly?"

"You were in it with a client of yours."

"I know exactly what you're referring to and it's not what it seems."

"What's the true story?"

He ran a hand over his hair, and then he

huffed. "It doesn't matter now. I want your parents' house for exactly the reason I said. I want to come here to relax. The place holds a lot of memories."

"I'm sorry, but that seems a little unbelievable. Why would it hold memories when you've never stepped a foot inside it?"

"If you must know, I used to go past it every weekend. I promised myself when I became successful I'd buy it. Now I've reached the stage where I consider myself just that and I'm fulfilling my childhood wish —or whim if you'd like to call it that."

She stared at him trying to figure out whether he was telling the truth.

"Beverly, does the place have any artifacts?"

"No. None that have been discovered." She felt foolish for ever thinking it had held artifacts merely because there was a cave on the property. It wasn't close to the other archaeological finds. They were miles away.

"Haven't you answered your own question?"

She nodded, feeling ashamed for doubting him. Maybe all his compliments had been genuine ones. She'd never been used to getting so many compliments. The Amish never mentioned a person's appearance, and even Kevin hadn't once told her she was attractive. "It doesn't change the fact that Jeremiah and Janet refuse to sell."

"Do you still doubt me?"

She hesitated.

"This has to be goodbye then, Beverly. I can't be involved with someone who doesn't believe me and doubts my every motive." He turned around and took a step away from her.

"Wait ... Oscar ... wait."

He turned around. "Yes?"

She licked her lips. It made sense to be with a man like Oscar. Then her world would be complete. They suited each other.

He was such a good catch...if he was genuine. But then there was David Hilty. If she'd stayed in the community, David would've been the kind of man she'd marry.

"Yes, Beverly?"

It was time. She had to make a decision. Immediately her analytical mathematical brain kicked in. Even though David was no longer available she had feelings for him and those feelings were more than the feelings she had for Oscar. What did her heart want? Which man did she love? It was David. It didn't matter that David was taken. She'd have to wait until she found that same feeling again with another man, and if she never did, she wouldn't settle for seconds. "Have a safe trip back to the city."

He glowered at her. "Is that it?"

She nodded.

Without wasting time, he walked to his car and she turned away from him. Then she heard him rev the engine of the Mercedes before he zoomed down the driveway and out of her life.

Her heart beat hard against her chest. Since David was already taken, had she just made the biggest mistake of her life? Should she have settled for Oscar? "Settled for." That said it all. She would've had a comfortable life, but she couldn't be with Oscar if she was still in love with David, even though he was taken. She heaved a sigh and tried to stop tears from falling. Why was her life always like this? Why couldn't she just be normal like other people? She didn't fit with the Amish and neither did she fit with the *Englisch.*

When she sat down on the couch, Janet joined her. "You sent him away I see?" She looked up at Janet with a nod. "You're crying?"

That only made Beverly cry more. "Janet, you should be mingling, talking to people."

"I've talked to everyone, and they're all

happily mingling with one another. You know, before I married your *vadder*, I had my own disappointments in love."

Beverly sniffed. "Did you?"

"*Ach jah.* I had three upsets. I was weeks away from marrying a man, Tom. I was nineteen and then he up and left the community."

"Oh, that's awful. I'm sorry."

"It was awful. I was devastated. My parents didn't understand. They told me I was better off without him and they said I should pull myself together."

Hearing about Janet's pain made her feel better about her own. "How long did it take for you to get over him?"

"Years. The next man in my life was Samuel Yoder. He was a widower with two small children. I ended things with him because a friend of mine told me that he wasn't really interested in me as a wife, that he just wanted a mother for the children."

"Was that true?"

Janet laughed. *"Nee.* She married him six months later."

"Oh no. I'm glad you can laugh. I would've been furious."

"As my *mudder* told me, the right man for me was still out there somewhere."

Beverly wiped her eyes. "What was the third one?"

"Ach, the third one wasn't as dramatic."

"Tell me."

"We were together, courting, for six months and then he ended things. That's when I met your *vadder* at a wedding. It was eighteen months after your *mudder* died."

Beverly nodded. "And *Dat* was your true love match?"

"Jah. He was the man I'd been waiting for."

"He really loves you."

"I know."

"It's funny how things work out. Well, not funny. It was horrible that my *mudder* died, but if she hadn't, who would you have married?"

"No one, I'd dare say."

"I was angry at God for so long for taking her away. And I'm sorry, but I was mad too that you married *Dat*."

Janet nodded. "I know, and I understood. I too had my own burdens to carry. He still loved your *mudder,* and you never accepted me, you were too old. I didn't blame you. Why should you accept the person who, you believed, took your *mudder's* place?"

More tears rolled down Beverly's face and Janet reached into her apron and passed her a handkerchief. Janet had broken down her barriers—the hardness protecting her heart was softening.

Beverly felt her own bitterness beginning to melt away. She wiped her cheeks and then dabbed at the corners of her eyes. "I'm so sorry; I was so horrible and mean to you."

Janet laughed. "You weren't so bad. I'm

sorry too. I'm sorry we couldn't have been closer. I've never had a child of my own."

"You wanted *kinner?*"

"Of course. Who wouldn't want to hold their own *boppli* in their arms?"

"I don't know. I think I could take it or leave it."

Janet chuckled as if she thought Beverly was joking. "There'd be no greater gift from *Gott.*"

"I'll probably never know how that feels either."

"Then we have something else in common."

Beverly smiled. "I guess so."

"I'm sorry about that lawyer, and about David."

After she had breathed in deeply, Beverly said, "It's okay. It will be okay."'"

"I think David had strong feelings for you, but he had a prior commitment."

No, he didn't! Beverly screamed in her

head. The woman left him, so they had no commitment. She'd cancelled her commitment. "I wonder if there would be work for me around here if I came back to the community."

"You'd really do that?" Janet asked.

"Yes. It would feel weird going back to my old life in the city now."

"You could work here helping me like you used to."

Beverly laughed. "No. *Denke,* but I'd want to work as a bookkeeper or something."

"Your *vadder* will be so happy."

Beverly put her finger up to her mouth. "Don't say anything to him just yet. I haven't fully made up my mind."

"You're very welcome to stay here."

She smiled at Janet. Now they were friends. How funny life was. They'd found a common bond in disappointment and sorrow. "I couldn't take up one of your rooms. I have a little money saved. I could buy a little apartment close by, or perhaps a small house."

"Build one on the land here. Your *vadder* would love that."

"Oh, I didn't even think of that. That would be wonderful." When Beverly watched Janet laugh, she saw her through new eyes. Janet no longer looked like a storybook witch. She looked more like a fairy god-mother, especially the way her silver-white spirals of hair framed her face like a halo.

"That's a buggy," Janet said.

"If it's all right. I'll go to my room. I'm in no mood for any of this." She looked around at the groups of people all eating and talking.

Janet nodded and Beverly trudged her way up the stairs. She closed herself in her room, glad that everyone had finished looking around the house. Minutes later, someone knocked on her door. She opened the door and saw her father standing there on his crutches. "Hello, *Dat*."

He looked around with a huge grin. "There you are. You know, I'm getting used to these things."

"Good. And you're doing so well with them."

"You didn't have to nag me."

"I didn't mean to, but someone's got to do it, I guess."

He laughed.

"You and Janet should be talking to people. The night's nearly over. We've had an excellent response."

Then she heard Janet calling her. That immediately annoyed her. She'd told Janet she couldn't face anyone. "What now?"

"Don't be so hard on her," her father said.

"Okay. Sorry."

She left her room and went to the top of the stairs. "Yes, Janet?"

"You have a visitor."

"Me?"

"*Jah.*"

A visitor? She hoped with all her heart it was David Hilty come back to tell her he couldn't live without her. Then reality reminded her that things like that didn't happen to a girl who had never fit in. She swallowed hard and made her way down the steps expecting to see the bishop, or perhaps Leah.

When she got to the bottom of the stairs she looked around, there was no Bishop Eli, or Leah... but there was her other good friend sitting on the couch.

"Betsy!"

"I'm back." Betsy laughed as Beverly ran to her.

The two girls hugged. Beverly was pleased to see her, but disappointed that it wasn't David. She took a step back. "I'm so happy you're here. I've only been here for a few weeks. And I'm just about to go back home. I've visited Leah and now it's so good to see you as well.

Where are your twins? I can't wait to see them."

"We're staying at Dora's. The twins are asleep and she told me you were here, so I've just stopped by quickly to say hello. We're here for a week, so please come see me."

Beverly bit her lip. "I don't know if I can."

"What's happening?"

She fought back another onslaught of tears and decided then and there to leave for good. The community was no place for her. Besides, if she came back to the community what kind of life would she have as a single woman? There'd be no life except going to work and coming back home, and then what? "Give me your address and I'll write to you. I'm going to go home tomorrow and I have a lot to do before I go."

"Tomorrow?"

"Yes."

"What's wrong? You look as though you're about to burst out crying."

She nodded. "I've had my share of upsets. I shouldn't have come back."

"I'm sorry to hear that. Is there anything I can do?"

"No. There's nothing anyone can do."

"You will write to me, won't you?"

Beverly nodded. "I'll give you my address and we can write to each other."

"I better get back to the twins. They're a bit of a handful for Dora to look after by herself. I didn't expect you'd have so many people here tonight."

"We did a bit of a refurbishment and this is the relaunch party."

"Ah." She looked around the room. "It's a lovely place. I've always liked it."

"Yes. Apparently, a lot of people do."

When everyone had left, Beverly slipped into the barn, made some calls and found out the bus schedule, and booked a taxi for the morning. After that, instead of going back to her room, she helped her father and Janet clean up. "I've decided I'm leaving tomorrow, *Dat.*"

He stopped still, placed the handful of dirty plates back down on the table and leaned over his crutches. His pale blue eyes widened. "I would prefer you stay, Petal."

"Beverly, you said you were going to stay."

"I know, but I can't. I'll see you next year when I've got vacation time built up again, okay?"

Jeremiah slowly nodded. "We're fine, don't you worry about us. Thanks to you, we've got people who've promised to spread the word. Everyone was impressed and the fellow from the newspaper is bringing back a photographer so he can write an article about the *haus.* The local tourist office is going to keep our brochures again. They said someone called and told them we were closed."

"Is that right?"

"*Jah.*"

It confirmed that something weird was going on. Who could've made that call and why? Oscar? One of the other two local bed-and-breakfast owners? Then she blamed herself. The first thing she should've done was visit the places that normally referred people, but she had been too fixated on her own problems. "It's good news about the news article. That's great news." She saw her father's eyes glaze over.

"I'm glad you came here, Beverly. Do you think you'll be able to help us?"

His mind was going again. "Yes, *Dat.* I think so."

Janet stepped forward. "She has helped us, Jeremiah. She has." She turned to Beverly. "I don't know what we would've done without you."

"I'm happy I was able to help."

"Do you need me to take you anywhere tomorrow?" Janet asked.

"Where are you going, Beverly?"

"I'm going home, but I'll come back and visit. Thanks, Janet, but everything's arranged. I've already booked a taxi."

Janet then turned to her husband. "You head off to bed, Jeremiah. I can do this."

"*Nee,* it's too much."

"Not for me. I once cooked for three hundred people by myself."

Beverly laughed. "I remember you told me that."

"What time are you leaving?" Janet asked.

"Around eight."

"Make sure you say goodbye."

"Of course I will."

After she'd helped Janet for another hour, they had the kitchen squared away. Beverly headed up to her room wondering why life had to be so hard. When was she ever going to be happy? She'd lost ten whole years with her father and now his mind was fading.

There was no way to get those precious years back again.

She'd thought David was her second chance until Susan showed up. And she also managed to drive Oscar away by being so suspicious. Her cheeks heated up at how stupid she was to think that Oscar, a successful New York lawyer, was skulking around caves looking for skeletons and artifacts. The good thing was, her visit back to her old community had cured her of constantly thinking about Kevin.

CHAPTER 20

THE NEXT MORNING, because she didn't like goodbyes, she waited in her room until the taxi pulled up to the house. When she was saying her brief goodbye, she knew her father was upset and even Janet looked a little sad.

Just as she was driving off in the taxi, she looked back at the house and then spotted something out of the ordinary—a man on her father's land. She leaned forward to speak to the driver. "Can you stop here a moment?"

He stopped the car, and she got out and headed over to the man. When she got closer she saw a yellow tripod and what looked like survey equipment. "Excuse me, do you mind telling me what you're doing?"

The balding short man turned around and looked at her, surprised. "Surveying."

"Yes, I can see that. For what?"

"The new owner's subdividing."

"Subdividing?"

"Yes. Into five acre lots."

"What new owner? My father owns this place. He hasn't sold it."

He pushed his lips tightly together as he studied Beverly. "Is that so?" he asked.

"Yes. It most definitely is."

He rustled through a bag of paperwork and read from it. "Cosgrove and Co Developments. That's the new owner."

"And would that company be owned by Oscar Reynolds?"

The man scratched his balding head.

"That's the man I've been dealing with. The sale's almost through and he wanted me to get an early start."

"Is that what he told you?"

The man nodded.

Beverly bit her lip. Her instincts had been right. "When did you last talk with him?"

"A couple of days ago."

"Well, you'd better call him and set him straight. No one ever agreed to sell to him. My father is not selling, and you'll need to leave the property. This land is not for sale!" She thought back to how hurt Oscar had acted and she couldn't believe it. He was quite the actor. When the man stood still staring at her, she said, "Call him right now if you don't believe me."

He walked a few paces away and pulled a phone from his pocket. After talking to someone on the phone, he ended the call and looked up at her. "The job's cancelled."

"That means you're trespassing."

"And that means I'm leaving." He hung his head and walked back to his equipment and it was then that Beverly saw his van parked down the side road.

She gave a sharp nod of her head. "Good."

"I'm very sorry about this. I just go where I'm sent."

"I understand." Beverly waited until he drove away and then she got back into the taxi, fuming about being thoroughly lied to by Oscar. There was one bright side, she was happy that she had trusted her gut and hadn't fallen for him. She could've made an awful mistake— another one.

The taxi continued toward the bus station, and she closed her eyes and prayed again that something good would happen in her life. She was through with being a misfit in society and never fitting in anywhere. When she opened her eyes, she decided she'd take more time off and discover what she really wanted in life. There had to be more than working and climbing the corporate ladder. Besides that, she had no degree and to go further in the bank she really needed one. The mere idea of the required years of study was daunting. She'd have to go to school while working full-time, and she wanted to enjoy life. Maybe the key was to take more vacations. She'd travel the world and visit lots of places.

"We're here, Miss."

Beverly was jolted out of her daydream. She handed some money over to the driver. "Thank you. Keep the change." She got out of the taxi and the driver met her around the back of the car to retrieve her one lonely suitcase. She took it from him and walked into the bus station, feeling very alone.

After a wait of three quarter of an hour, the boarding for her bus was called over the loudspeaker. She stood up and picked up her suitcase and then heard someone call her name. She swung around and saw David hurrying toward her.

She hoped he was there because he couldn't live without her. Then she had a déjà vu moment and remembered the disappointment she had felt ten years ago when she'd been certain her father had come to take her back home. Her father had only come to give her money and wish her well. She steeled her heart for another disappointment.

"What are you doing here?" she asked, looking around to see if Susan was close by.

"Where are you going?"

She looked around at the people getting on her bus and then back to him. "I'm going back to my life in the city."

"Don't go. I don't want to lose you."

She froze. "What are you saying?"

His face lit up and his eyes sparkled. "I'm pretty certain I love you, Beverly."

She stared at him, scarcely believing what she heard. "Aren't you marrying, Susan?"

"*Nee.*" He shook his head. "I can't marry anyone else when there's only one woman in my heart."

"Me?"

He smiled and nodded. "*Jah,* you. Stay with me?" He held out his hand. "Would you consider coming back to the community and marrying me? After a suitable time has passed, of course."

A giggle escaped her lips as her free hand flew to her mouth. Her heart sang. That was what she wanted more than anything. The call for her bus came once more. She'd trusted Kevin once. Could she trust another man not to change his mind?

"Do you have to think about it?" he asked, letting his hand fall back down by his side. "It's okay."

"What if you change your mind?"

"I often change my mind, but I'll never change my mind about you."

"But what about Susan?"

He sighed. "It was only out of a sense of obligation that I went away with her. I was trapped, and couldn't bear to hurt her. I didn't know if I could offer you the life that you wanted." He drew a breath. "Susan knew. She said I didn't look at her the way I looked when I spoke about you. She told me to find you and tell you how I feel, and once I was released from my commitment, here I am."

"She said that?"

"She did. Will you consider—"

Right there in the middle of the station, she dropped her suitcase to the ground and collapsed into him, leaning against him. His arms encircled her and held her close. "You'll come back with me?" he whispered into her ear.

"I will."

"The next question is, 'Will you marry me?'"

She giggled. "And the answer is, I will."

After a quiet moment, he said, "Let's go back and tell Jeremiah and Janet."

She didn't want anything to ruin her moment. "Can't we keep this to ourselves?"

He chuckled. *"Nee.* I want to shout it from the highest mountain, and we have to give them a reason for you coming back, don't we?"

She smiled. "I guess we'll have to tell them. They'll be pleased, I hope."

"I hope so, too."

As they walked out of the station arm-in-arm, David carrying her suitcase, she asked, "Where will we live?"

"Anywhere you want. I can sell my half of the sawmill to my *bruder* if you want to stay close to your folks. He's willing to buy it from me."

"You've already asked him?"

He chuckled. "I have."

"You thought I'd say yes?"

"I was hoping. And I've kind of got a liking for this bed-and-breakfast business."

"Want to know a secret?"

"What's that?" he asked.

"So have I."

They both laughed.

When they arrived back at the house, Janet opened the door and when she saw Beverly, her jaw nearly hit the floor.

"Surprise! I'm back."

Janet looked from Beverly to David and then back to Beverly. "I can see that."

From the look on Janet's face she'd figured out what was going on.

Beverly stared at David hoping he would break the news, so she wouldn't have to.

"Beverly and I have something to tell you and Jeremiah."

Janet's eyebrows nearly flew to the top of her white prayer *kapp.* "Right now?"

"*Jah,* if he's awake?"

"He is. He's in the living room. Come in." She ushered them both inside and soon they were all gathered in the living room.

"What have I done to deserve such a crowd in here today? And why are you back so soon, Beverly? Haven't you left yet?"

Once again Beverly looked at David.

"Beverly has agreed to marry me."

Jeremiah smoothed down his beard. "Is that so?"

"Yes, it's true. I'm coming back to the community and in time, when the bishop allows it, David and I will be married."

"Are you sure?" her father asked.

It worried her that her father asked that question. "Of course I'm sure."

His face broke into a smile and he immediately looked years younger. "Then that's the happiest news I've heard since you walked back into this *haus*."

She looked at Janet to see if she would be happy too, and saw her stepmother's eyes were moist. Immediately, tears filled her own.

"I'm sorry for any heartache I've brought you both over the years. I didn't mean to."

"There, there. No harm done. We'll all have a new start. How's that?" Janet's lips curled upward and her face softened.

"Yes, I'd like a new start."

"Will you stay here?" Jeremiah asked.

David said, "That might be something we can discuss with you later."

"Janet, from tomorrow, I'm driving the buggy."

"That's too soon, Jeremiah."

"*Nee*, it's not. I feel stronger now."

Janet nodded. "If you think you can do it. You can start slowly."

Beverly said, "I've got some loose ends to

tie up in the city. I have to give notice at my job, and let my apartment go."

"Don't you come back with those horrid pink nails," Janet said with a silly grin.

Beverly giggled. "I won't."

"You won't be away too long, will you?" David asked

She looked into David's eyes. "I'll be back as soon as I possibly can. Once I've given my notice, I don't think they'll care if I leave right away. My assistants are well trained, so if my boss agrees, I could be back within a week."

"It'll be a very long week," David said.

FOUR MONTHS after Beverly got baptized into the Amish faith, she and David stood before the bishop as he pronounced them husband and wife.

The only sadness that pricked Beverly's

heart was that her mother was not there on her special day, but perhaps she was looking down upon her. She glanced around at her father who was recovered from his leg fracture but continuing to show his age, and the faithful Janet who was always by her husband's side. Beverly blinked rapidly. If she started crying, she wouldn't be able to stop.

It was later, during the wedding breakfast, that Janet pulled her aside. "Beverly, I've saved something for you."

"What is it?"

"I found it many years ago and I put it away for a day like this. When you left us all those years ago, I didn't think you were coming back, but I hung onto it just the same. *Gott* heard me."

"You prayed for me to come back?"

"*Jah,* and now here it is, your wedding day. The day I never thought would happen."

Beverly giggled. "You and me both." Beverly wondered what she was hiding behind her back.

"Do you want to see it?"

"*Jah,* you have me intrigued."

From behind her back, she produced the old recipe scrapbook. The one that had gone missing soon after Janet had married Jeremiah.

Beverly's mouth fell open. "That was *Mamm's.*"

Janet handed it over. "I know, that's why I saved it for you. You were always leafing through it and I was afraid you'd damage it before you realized its true value."

"You hid it?"

"*Jah.* I knew you'd appreciate it when you got older."

Tears filled Beverly's eyes as she hugged the book to her heart. She was ashamed of herself for thinking Janet had thrown it in the trash. Janet wasn't as evil as she had imagined. "I didn't know where it had gone.

Thank you for putting it away for me. Now it's as nice as the last time I saw it."

"I kept it safe. I hope you can cook lovely things from it for your family." Janet smiled sweetly.

"I will. I definitely will." Beverly held the book in one hand and opened her arms wide to hug the stepmother who had been big-hearted enough to love a young and reluctant stepdaughter despite the child's grief and anger.

Janet turned then and walked away, leaving Beverly staring at the book. They might never be best friends, but now Beverly knew that Janet's heart was in the right place. She turned around and looked at her father who was talking to David. Jeremiah had asked Beverly and David to take over the bed-and-breakfast, with Janet's full agreement. David was already in the process of adding on to the main house, so they'd have their own private rooms.

It was the perfect life. Beverly would run the business side, Janet would do all the cooking, and David's domain would be the maintenance and gardening with Jeremiah providing whatever help he could. They had agreed to keep Dora on staff for the house-keeping. If God blessed them with children, both Beverly and David would be home with them, as would their grandparents.

As for Oscar Reynolds, they hadn't seen or heard from him since, and according to the locals he'd never lived in the valley as he'd told them. The only thing the locals knew about him was that he was trying to buy property to subdivide and resell, and he truly had once tried to purchase properties on behalf of someone else, despite his denials.

TWO YEARS after Beverly and David's marriage they were blessed with their first child, a boy they named Jeremiah David Hilty. Two years after that, they were blessed with a girl, Ruth Janet, named after the two women who'd shaped Beverly's life. The relationship between herself and Janet continued to mend, helping to heal both of their wounded hearts.

Beverly knew that God had seen the end from the beginning and that He'd had a plan for goodness and blessing. She still didn't know why her mother had to leave her, but accepted that some things were beyond her limited reasoning. If she hadn't left the community when she did, she might not have met David on her return and with her former experiences in love, she appreciated David even more.

Finally, Beverly had found a place where she fit just right. With God in her heart and David and her children by her side, and the gift of being close to her father in his old age, Beverly was settled in a place where she fit in —a place she could finally call home.

Trust in the LORD with all thine heart;
and lean not unto thine own understanding.
Proverbs 3:5

Thank you for reading Jeremiah's Daughter.

THE NEXT BOOK IN THE SERIES

Book 7 Amish Misfits
My Brother's Keeper.

Amy's life revolves around caring for Jonah, her beloved special needs brother. When Adam, a visitor residing with the neighboring bishop, offers his assistance despite his lack of understanding about Jonah's condition, Amy is skeptical.
However, as their paths intertwine, Amy's initial reservations begin to wane, and she

finds herself drawn to Adam in unexpected ways. As their connection deepens, Amy's heart wrestles with the truth behind Adam's stay with the bishop.

AMISH MISFITS

Book 7 My Brother's Keeper

Book 8 The Amish Marriage Pact

ABOUT SAMANTHA PRICE

Samantha Price is a USA Today bestselling and Kindle All Stars author of Amish romance books and cozy mysteries. She was raised Brethren and has a deep affinity for the Amish way of life, which she has explored extensively with over a decade of research.

She is mother to two pampered rescue cats, and a very spoiled staffy with separation issues.

SamanthaPriceAuthor.com

ALL SAMANTHA PRICE'S SERIES

Amish Maids Trilogy

Amish Love Blooms

Amish Misfits

The Amish Bonnet Sisters

Amish Women of Pleasant Valley

Ettie Smith Amish Mysteries

Amish Secret Widows' Society

Expectant Amish Widows

Seven Amish Bachelors

Amish Foster Girls

Amish Brides

Amish Romance Secrets

Amish Christmas Books

Amish Wedding Season

Made in the USA
Monee, IL
23 November 2024

71010668R20184